W9-BUP-783

i

THE GOLDEN CHANCE

Also published in Large Print
from G.K. Hall by T. V. Olsen:

Keno
Starbuck's Brand
Track the Man Down

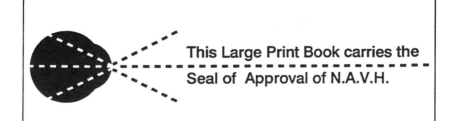

**This Large Print Book carries the
Seal of Approval of N.A.V.H.**

THE GOLDEN CHANCE

T. V. Olsen

G.K. Hall & Co.
Thorndike, Maine

Published in Large Print by arrangement with
Golden West Literary Agency.

G.K. Hall Large Print Book Series.

Set in 16 pt. News Plantin by Juanita Macdonald.

Printed in the United States on acid-free,
high-opacity paper. ∞

Library of Congress Cataloging in Publication Data

Olsen, Theodore V.
   The golden chance / T.V. Olsen.
      p.   cm.
   ISBN 0-8161-5861-4 (alk. paper : lg. print)
   1. Large type books. I. Title.
  [PS3565.L8G6 1993]
  813'.54—dc20   93-27028

THE GOLDEN CHANCE

CHAPTER ONE

As he prowled along a southwest bend of the Los Pinos River, Gage Cameron wasn't looking for gold.

He was just hunting through the tangles of dense hazelnut brush and rabbit runs that laced the high ground above the steep, crumbling bank worn down by the Los Pinos in its centuries of boiling through a wide channel below. Gage wasn't looking for anything except to bag a cottontail or two for supper. A man grew tired of a steady diet of beef or mutton. Or even mountain-stream trout, which could easily be caught in the quiet eddies of backwater a ways upriver.

Intent on his stalking, Gage was only half-aware that he had edged from a solid rimrock onto softer ground. And then it was too late, as a shelving section of the bank gave way under his feet.

Quick as a cat, Gage Cameron flung himself sideways toward solid ground, at the same time pitching his rifle away from him and grabbing out with both hands. All he was able to seize was handfuls of collapsing dirt. Then he was plunging straight down through a small avalanche till his body slammed against the hard but almost sheer slope. He slid a few feet farther before his fingers hooked in and brought him to a stop.

With his face pressed against the dirt, Gage barely heard, above the roar of water below, the rattle of sand and pebbles raining into the river. Carefully, coughing and spitting dirt, he turned his head and peered down. If he relaxed his hold, he would be dumped for about fifty feet into a roiling, rock-studded current, for the Los Pinos ran shallow at this point.

Could he clamber upward?

Above him, prospects seemed not much better. The sloughed-away section of rim still left a precarious slope to be negotiated, and the soil was loose. Here he was clinging to a mere shallow protuberance of rock, and his legs were dangling free.

Gage kicked inward, groping with his feet till he located an unseen toehold. Now he could brace his weight, but how long could he hold on? Frantically he reached up as far as he could with one hand, scrabbling about in the dirt.

His fingers found another jutting point of rock. He reached up with the other hand and clutched it, exerting his full strength to pull himself a few inches higher, but only by giving up his toeholds.

Still farther above was another jutting edge of rock. He extended his other arm and took hold and hoisted himself on and up. Raw pain arrowed through his arms and shoulders as he grabbed still higher. Again he pulled himself up. He did the same thing once more. Now, by doubling his legs, Gage was able to plant his booted toes on the projecting rock lip that had first stopped his fall.

Maybe . . . maybe he could make it. Better than chancing the battering descent that lay below.

The caved-in cutbank above leaned inward a little now. Choosing his holds with infinite care, using his sense of touch rather than sight, he went on upward, his boots digging in hard.

Gage looked back over his shoulder, blinking against the wash of sweat and grit in his eyes. Through the stinging blur, he made out three men sitting on their horses on a rise of ground above the opposite bank of the river.

The land wasn't nearly as high on that side, tapering down to the tumbling rush of the Los Pinos. His watering eyes could barely pick them out, three dark shapes against the lightness of sky above a dark horizon. Cautiously he lowered one hand to rub his sleeve over his face and eyes once in order to clear his sight, then swiftly resumed his handhold. At this distance all he could make out for sure was that they were a trio of white men, teeth showing chalk white in their faces, laughing, joshing about his predicament.

It was funny as hell, all right. They weren't friendly, and he was helpless, clinging like a fly to his precarious holds.

Gage saw one man yank a rifle from his saddle scabbard. As he lifted it, the rider alongside him reached out and batted the piece down, saying something but grinning as he said it.

Jesus. Gage was like a sitting duck where he

was, and he realized they were set to have some fun with him. The men spoke briefly, then yelled at him some more. He could imagine a few of the taunting words. Such as *breed* and *Injun* and *siwash*.

He could guess what brand they rode for, too.

The one raised his rifle again, and this time the man alongside made no move to stop him. He and the third man were also unlimbering their rifles.

Doggedly, gritting his teeth, Gage began to haul himself upward again. A bullet whanged off naked rock less than a foot from his right elbow, followed by the ringing echo of the shot.

They began laying down a regular fusillade of gunfire.

The slugs whined off rocks and plowed fans of dirt against him. They were shooting as close to him as they dared without hitting him. The din of shots merged as a single roar above the rushing water.

He froze where he was, hugging the escarpment, chin bent against his chest. Dirt, pebbles, and chips of rock pelted against his body.

Gage Cameron felt a seething rage that drowned even the panic rising in him. He could feel the numbing strain on his arms creeping deeper into his shoulders and back. He knew he couldn't hold on for more than a few moments longer. . . .

Suddenly the rock to which he was clinging tore free of the soil. It nearly came down on his head, tearing his right ear, bashing against his shoulder before it plunged on.

Gage was plunging, too, his grip torn away. This time his raw fingers and numbed muscles could gain no purchase to stop his descent. He was in a free-fall for a couple of seconds before his body jarred against an outcrop. The impact drove the breath from his lungs. He kept falling down the almost sheer slope, caroming off several rocks that smashed against his trunk and arms and legs. He had the presence of mind to clasp both arms tightly around his ducked head to save his skull. Only the spaces of softer ground and scrub vegetation between rocks cushioned his descent a little.

He landed facedown and lay motionless, his arms still hugging his head as residual dirt and stones cascaded over his prone form and into the water.

He'd been brought up about a foot short of the river's edge by slides of rubble that had fallen from above. His whole body throbbed like one enormous bruise. After a few aching moments he rolled slowly onto his back, tensed for an agony of broken bones.

Miraculously he felt none. Not even a crushed rib as his fingers explored for one. With a vast and painful effort, Gage was able to sit up. Dumbly he watched his hat bobbing away down the rapids. His hands were bleeding but still numb. He felt a hot crawl of blood down his neck from the torn ear; blood from minor cuts patched his clothing. He dropped a hand into the foaming water and gingerly scrubbed his eyes clean.

He squinted up at the far bank. The three men were laughing uproariously as they reined their horses around. They rode away across the rise without a backward glance and were lost to sight.

Gage braced his bloody hands against the slide rubble and pushed shakily to his feet, wincing but not making a sound. The rage he felt was too deep and consuming to permit any release by cursing. He didn't have a shred of doubt that the bastards would have been as willing to put a slug into him as near him, if not for the telltale bullet hole in his corpse.

Finally he was able to heave himself onto his feet. He swayed back and forth as he opened his bloody fists. They were clenched around handfuls of dirt he had clutched in the effort of getting up.

He opened his hands and watched the dirt drip from them. The shock that ran through him almost drove the pain from his mind.

Sweet Jesus.

Micalike sparkles danced off the soil spattered around his feet. But it wasn't mica. The midday sun struck yellowish glimmers from the flakes.

Gold?

Gage Cameron dropped to his raw knees, digging his fingers into the earth. Almost at once he uncovered a sizable nugget of the stuff. He dipped it in the water and rubbed it. A gulp of in-held breath whistled from his lungs.

It has to be.

He began digging with a frantic haste, and yet carefully, into the slide rubble, both the fresh and the old. He sifted each handful through his fingers. He found loose gold ranging from small particles to more nuggets of a respectable size.

He rocked back on his haunches, staring for a long moment at his find, then tipping his gaze upward. If this much lay under his feet in the rubble, it must have fallen from above. There must be more — who could say how much? — embedded in the escarpment.

For right here alone, Gage was certain, he must be squatting on hundreds of dollars' worth of raw treasure.

CHAPTER TWO

Almost at once, Gage managed to clamp a brake on his exultance.

Maybe because he was only half Indian and only half his upbringing had been Indian. At one time the Navaho had had no use for the white man's wealth, which they'd viewed with contempt, except for his trade wares. They wrought ornately in silver design and ornamentation, but were only starting to use the stuff as currency. The more they rubbed against the white man, the better they absorbed his capacity for naked greed.

But gold . . . gold was what really inflamed the whites. They would lie, steal, cheat, kill for a few ounces of it. Gage was usually a cautious sort anyway, and caution flagged down his first reaction.

He picked up handfuls of the dirt and dribbled it through his fingers, automatically sorting out the golden flakes and nuggets, piling them to one side. For all his outward calm, he could feel his heart pounding, his breathing labored.

Christ . . . he was a wealthy man, if the stuff proved out as he hoped. He'd have to make sure of that. A man could be misled by pyrites —

fool's gold — and other worthless minerals. Lots of people had been misled, to their everlasting regret.

But there was no halter on Gage's imagination.

God, what this could mean for his family! For his younger brother and sister, who had turned out to be — so far — a pair of sorry specimens. He'd see to it they were set on a sound path, by doling out the wealth only in slow dribbles. He thought fleetingly and sorrowfully of his father, Mungo Cameron. Likely it was too late to rehabilitate old Mungo. He'd been awash in booze for so many years that it would take a miracle to straighten him out.

That's why they'd all lived in poverty for so long. Gage had done his best to hold his slovenly clan together, but a man might as well shout at the sky. Carefully used, his accidental find could turn their fortunes around. . . .

Gage separated the gold and dirt as well as he could, then turned his attention to the escarpment above. He stood up and dug into it a little, dislodging chunks of earth and rock with his bare hands. He found no sign of gold as high as he could reach. But if it had fallen from higher up, he would find it in time.

He knew he had to have patience and maintain utter secrecy. He'd have to make his plans carefully. This spot lay wide open to anyone who chanced to come up on the far bank, as those three riders had. But it was isolated enough by the river's breadth to have escaped discovery till now.

Gage peeled off his shirt, gathered his small store of precious metal into it, and knotted up the sleeves.

He paused to splash more cold water over his head and cuts, slung the loaded shirt across his shoulder, and started tramping upstream along the narrow band of rubble, going slowly because he was limping some and the rubble sloped unevenly. He was aware of a hundred bruising aches through his body, and it couldn't dull his buoyancy. Somewhat surprised at how heavy the little bundle was, he remembered what he had heard and read about the inordinate weight of gold. *Must be the real thing!*

Gage wondered idly what the three riders had been doing at this far western end of RBJ property. It held little in the way of proper graze. Not likely they'd be combing the brush for strays in midsummer. Simply bad timing that they'd come on him — or damned good timing from his viewpoint, after all. There was the gold. . . .

He tramped steadily for about a half hour. The rapids began diminishing to deep pools formed where natural dams of boulders contained the water. He passed beneath a shelving overhang ledge where he and the kids had always liked to go swimming, diving into the water, or just sunning themselves. Only a little farther now and he could climb out.

Gage was sweating profusely from a growing weariness composed of his burden, the battering punishment his body had taken, and his awkwardness on the shifting, uneven fall of rubble. Several times he slipped and nearly fell into the water. The Los Pinos grew wider, and finally, at a point where the escarpment fell gradually away to a sandy, shallow beach, he was able to climb out.

He laid down the gold and dropped on his haunches, panting and perspiring. A short rest and he would work back downriver to where he'd left his horse before ranging afoot through the brush, hunting for rabbits. But all thought of bagging game was gone. Hide the gold and return for it later and look for more.

In the way of a man accustomed to the wilds, Gage mechanically took in his surroundings. Almost at once he saw the uniform depressions etched into the sand by shod hooves some five yards away. He got up and plodded over for a closer look.

No doubt about it. Three riders had forded the river here; it ran only a foot deep at this place and the current was sluggish, almost placid. He could also pick out where the men had descended the bank on the far side.

It had to be the trio of RBJ men. They had crossed here, riding off their native range deliberately. They'd purposefully aimed for this fording spot, and the close-grouped tracks heading away showed they were in a moderate hurry.

Gage wondered why. His scalp prickled with a sixth sense, his curiosity aroused. This might bear some investigation. Also, he owed those RBJ

17

bastards something. He wanted to pay it off.

Straightening up from his study of the ground, Gage Cameron was a medium-tall young man in his late twenties. His features and gleaming brown skin showed the predominance of his Navaho mother's blood. His body was almost gauntly lean and tightly knit; shirtless, his trunk didn't show an ounce of superfluous flesh; his arms were corded with long, lithe muscle. The white-worn fray of his old Levi's clung to his whittled hips and catty flanks; his feet were shod in stiff-soled moccasins with upcurled toes. Cinched around his waist was a silver-worked belt of Navaho make; it supported a beaded sheath with a bone-handled hunting knife. His face was broad and yet bony, bisected by a broad wedge of a nose; his hair was jet black, coarse as a horse's mane, and hung nearly to his shoulders. His black eyes and straight mouth rarely revealed his thoughts, but right now both hinted at a hard, cold determination.

Shouldering his burden again, Gage began the downriver walk along the rim. This time he had a sight easier going, pausing only to retrieve the rifle he had thrown into the brush. In a few minutes he came to where he had left his horse ground-hitched in the chaparral. The roan gelding pawed the ground and nickered a soft greeting. Gage set down his load with a snort of relief and stood by the roan for a moment. Murmuring the Navaho horse-calming word *ho-shuh* as he sheathed the Winchester in its scabbard, he leaned a hand on the saddle, resting and thinking.

Where to cache the gold? In quantity what he'd taken amounted to little; it could easily be concealed. But he wanted to be absolutely sure the place would remain his secret, his alone.

The old Navaho camp — that was it.

The tumbledown ruins of a cluster of earth lodges or hogans lay just a little back from the escarpment where he'd fallen. Overgrown by brush, for it had been deserted for many years, it was entirely shunned by the Navaho and by whites as well.

Gage suspended the bundle of gold from his saddle horn and struck off into the brush, leading the roan. He came almost at once on the grisly remains of the old camp.

The Navaho had never formed villages, although they sometimes planted corn and peach trees and a few vegetables in the manner of the Hopi. They'd move about in family groups and would occasionally set up dwellings presided over by a mother and her married daughters. More scattered lodges were built of brush and erected anywhere that flocks of sheep might be grazed. Gage's own clan — his mother's — had set up this camp sometime before a flare of smallpox had wiped out all but a few of them.

The old-time Navaho had not buried their dead; they would simply abandon the dwelling place. Rarely would they touch a dead body, even that of a slain enemy. This custom was born of superstitious dread — fear both of the dead and of shaman-inspired witchcraft. The survivors of this camp had fled it long ago, and nobody ventured near it anymore. These were *tchindi betatakin* — death hogans.

Nobody ventured near, except a well-schooled half-breed like Gage Cameron, who had discarded his own people's beliefs in boyhood, though he had little use for white man's customs and beliefs either, save as convenience sometimes dictated.

Just the sight of the old, collapsed hogans, the scatter of broken pottery, abandoned tools, gray and tattered bits of cloth and blankets, and all the desiccated or (mostly) skeletal remains of corpses was enough to discourage curiosity. Wolves and coyotes had done their scavenging, leaving a wide clutter of bones, some of them half buried in the sand among the brush and weeds.

Gage threw the gelding's reins and unslung the bundle of gold, then tramped forward a few yards till he found the object he was looking for — a bleached skull that lay partly buried in sand but tipped sideways so that only half its grotesque gap-toothed grin was visible.

It was a marker he couldn't forget. The first time he'd seen it, the skull had badly disconcerted him. Now it only touched him with a barren and ironic amusement that his granduncle Adakhai, the venerable and (he thought) half-dotty shaman, deplored in him. The old man always chided his grandnephew's skepticism, warning that in time the Vanished Old Ones would pay off his scorn in kind.

Gage grinned back at the skull, knelt beside it, and began to scoop a narrow hole in the earth. He ran into hard clay a few inches down and continued to dig, separating the clay and sand. Then he unknotted his shirt and, after singling out a few nuggets to stuff in his pocket, dumped its contents in the hole. He packed the clay back above it and sifted the dry sand over the clay, arranging it so that the site blended into the surrounding soil.

"You stand guard right pert, old bonehead," he told the skull, again returning its half grin. He backed away from the spot in a crouch, neatly erasing his own tracks with his hand. A few yards away, he rose to his feet and shrugged into his grimy shirt, then swung back toward the roan.

A stir of cold air breathed over him, canceling the afternoon warmth.

Gage halted, looking around him. Pieces of gray and torn cloth blew across the bare ground, whipped up as though by a rising wind. It riffled the brush, clattering the wands of branches. A tumbleweed blew against his legs. Gage looked quickly upward. The sun was brassy-bright in a cloudless sky, and beyond the camp no brush stirred at all.

This was no ordinary wind. Its sound grew to a thin whistling underscored by a strange moaning note. And it held a gray chill that seeped through his flesh and into his bones.

Suddenly the roan let out a high-pitched whinny; it reared back stiff-legged. Gage grabbed at the trailing reins, too late. The animal wheeled and bolted away through the brush.

Gage stood frozen to the spot, staring wildly about him, half expecting to see something. But there was nothing. Only the wind-thrashed brush, the chill blast of air that reached to his marrow.

Then it ceased — as abruptly as it had come. Silence. The sun shone brightly all around. The brush was motionless in a drowsing summer warmth.

Gage looked at the skull again. The sand around it had blown away enough to almost fully expose its grimacing grin.

Jesus! Gage made his muscles move. He was unsteady on his feet as he pushed back through the brush. He gave a piercing whistle which usually served to summon the roan.

The animal was nowhere in sight, but he followed its tracks till they showed the horse slowing toward a stop. Gage whistled again. Receiving no response, he pushed on through the chaparral.

He found the roan in a tight clearing. It shied away from his approach. *"Ho-shuh. ho-shuh,"* Gage said gently. The animal's eyes were rolling wildly, showing the whites; slobber streaked the edges of its mouth. But it stood unmoving as he came up and slowly grasped the reins. He laid his hand on the roan's neck, feeling the nervous jitter of its muscles. It was trembling all over. He touched the roached mane, and it seemed to bristle unnaturally.

Whatever had terrified his mount must be akin

to what he felt himself. If what had happened had been only some wild vagary of his own imagination, some residue of an early upbringing steeped in superstition, why would the horse feel it, too?

Still badly shaken, but not enough to succumb to the near-panic that gripped him. Gage climbed into his saddle and nudged the horse into motion on a careful rein. He didn't want to risk spooking it again.

All he wanted was to get away from this place as fast as he could.

CHAPTER THREE

Gage rode back toward the shallow fording of the Los Pinos, trying to push the eerie experience out of his thoughts. He knew that a completely rational man would try to fix on a rational explanation alone. Maybe he could even come up with one. But Gage was no scientist or philosopher. A realist, maybe — in that he'd always believed only in what he could verify through his own senses.

Yet maybe, at rare times, the irrational *was* the reality.

The hell with it. For now.

Coming to the tracks where the three riders had crossed the river, Gage swung the roan gelding up the sandy bank and onto the prairie bunchgrass. Here the trail was less plain, but he could still follow it on horseback, bending from his saddle to discern the pressed grasses. Following track easily where an ordinary man would be baffled was almost second nature to him.

It was too beautiful a Wyoming day to be thinking of either the occult or the violent. The carpets of rich green rose and fell with the slight undulations of land, and they were stippled with bluebells, larkspur, delphinium, a dozen pastel hues of pink, blue, and lavender. Ancient crags worn to shape by time and weather poked out here and there, and in places the shallow soil bristled with toughly twisted scrub trees, pines, and junipers. The sun lay hot and heavy against his left side; the sky was a cloudless arch of cobalt blue. Even the thick afternoon heat was passably comfortable as long as a man held a slow pace. The roan had almost calmed down except for an occasional spasm of muscle tremor.

The three riders had been heading for a definite objective. They'd leisurely skirted around crags and timber stands but held to a pretty definite north-by-northwest direction. Gage kept more alert than usual. Mounted men were easier to track than animals; usually they were less wary than animals. But well-armed men could also be a hell of a lot more dangerous.

His senses grew even sharper when he came onto the well-defined ruts left by wheels of a spring wagon. The tracks ran roughly north and south, both coming and going. Where the three riders had transected the ruts, they had followed them north.

The sun was heeling deeper toward the west, the shadows growing longer, when he rode up a long, grassy rise and caught a drift of faint sound from beyond it. Men's voices? He dismounted, took his field glasses from a saddlebag, and lifted his Winchester from its scabbard, then continued upward on foot, leading the gelding.

The summit of the rise was bearded with scattered mottes of brush. Now Gage could plainly pick out the voices at some little distance. He left the gelding and loped up to the crest and through the brush, moving in easy silence. Halting when his vantage brought a clear view of what lay below and beyond, he saw a small and crude-looking cabin built of rough timbers but made snug by "clay cat" chinking wedged between the logs. A completed brush corral lay on a downslope, along with an open-sided hay shed and a couple of smaller half-finished buildings.

Gage took in all this at a glance. What riveted his attention was five people in the yard. Two of the three riders were still mounted; the third was on foot, wielding a long bullwhip. He was using it on a man who had been roped by the two on horseback, one on each side of him. Their lariats were pulled taut, dallied around their saddle horns, so that the man was almost helplessly immobile. Yet he was struggling wildly, his arms pinned to his sides.

His shirt hung in bloody ribbons. The man afoot was lashing him, the whip peeling forward and backward in measured powerful strokes, cracking around the man's torso. At each blow he jerked like a puppet on strings. His teeth were a smear of white, bared with pain in his dark face. But he didn't let out a sound.

Neither did the woman. She lay off to one side, her hands and feet bound.

Gage set the field glasses to his eyes. The man and woman were both black. The three riders

26

were the only ones making any sound, shouting with the pleasurable excitement of this diversion. Taunting the black man as they had taunted Gage himself.

The rider now on foot was easy to recognize. A tall, pale-haired man, broad-shouldered and narrow-hipped, lithe and strong, his grin holding a fierce frenzy. Thaddeus Overmile . . . the nephew of RBJ's owner. Gage didn't know the two mounted men right off, but he didn't waste even a moment trying to identify them.

Gage Cameron's blood boiled with an instant and instinctive fury.

He dropped the glasses, raised the Winchester to his shoulder, sighted in briefly, and pulled off three quick shots. Two bullets kicked up clods next to the forefeet of the mounted men's horses. The third spattered dirt over the bullwhipper's boots.

Thaddeus Overmile stopped yelling. He was caught flat-footed, totally stunned. His startled glance raked along the high brush, picking out the blanket of powder smoke, but not Gage, who was nearly concealed by the tall thicket from which he'd fired.

Gage laid down another shot close to the man's feet, then bounded away, slithering down the brush-strewn slope on a sideways course, always keeping himself noiselessly out of sight.

The three men reacted swiftly now.

The mounts were fiddle-footing crazily, and their two riders dropped out of their saddles, unsheathing their rifles. Thad Overmile threw the whip aside and ran over to his own horse, almost spooking it as he tore his rifle from the scabbard. He did a kind of scared hobbling dance to one side as he cocked the piece.

Immediately the three men opened fire at the broad smudge of fraying gun smoke, but Gage was already crouching behind a dense thicket yards away. From here he poured a rapid random fire around the three, never trying to hit one, although he was sorely tempted.

Again he shifted position, this time fading up-slope a bit. Again he sent off several shots. The men below had already riddled his first position, and now they opened up with another wild volley at his second one, even as Gage fired from his third.

Then they panicked.

An instant after Thad Overmile's command to "get the hell out of here," his men were back in saddle, spurring their horses into flight.

Thad started running back for his horse. Gage shot the heel off his right boot. He'd aimed just ahead of him, but the chance result was even more satisfying. The slug sent Thad's boot heel flying as if ejected by a spring. The force crossed his running legs in midstride and sent him plowing on his face in a skidding sprawl.

Thaddeus scrambled to his feet, his face scraped bloody, and flung himself across his horse, kicking into a run even before he was securely in saddle. Gage had been counting his shots. Aiming care-

28

fully now, he knocked one of the fleeing men's hats spinning from his head.

That was Gage's last load. He watched the bloodied black man swaying on his feet, looking bewilderedly upward as he shed the ropes. Always cautious, Gage retreated invisibly back up the slope to his horse and methodically reloaded the Winchester, thumbing shells from a saddlebag into its fifteen-load magazine.

Afterward he strode out into plain sight of the people below. The black man had turned to stand dazedly watching the three riders drop out of sight beyond another rise. Now he shook himself like a big bear and plodded over to where the woman lay tied hand and foot.

Gage called to them as he started down the long slope, holding his rifle above his head in a token of friendship or at least neutrality.

The two stared for a long moment at their unexpected savior, and then the man finished untying the woman. Both were on their feet, unsteadily supporting each other, warily eyeing Gage as he tramped into the yard.

A baby was crying inside the cabin. The woman pulled away and stumbled inside. The man stood rubbing his arms, blinking, as Gage came up to him.

"Man," he said, "was you the only one? I thought it was an army cut loose up there."

"Maybe those gentlemen thought so, too," Gage said. "I was moving around some. Name's Gage Cameron."

"Reeve Bedoe," the man said, thrusting out his hand. "Man, I tell you, I am owing you. . . ." He gripped Gage's hand and turned his head, calling, "Opal?"

The woman came out of the doorway, holding a baby to her breast, patting its head, crooning soothingly. The infant's cries had ebbed to a few whimpers and a mild hiccuping.

"Reeve, are you all right?" she asked.

"Naw. I kin stand, though. That man didn't break nothing but my hide, far as I can tell."

"I'll put some liniment on those . . . those cuts."

"A mite later. Make it whiskey. No damn horse liniment. Whiskey, a man can massage his insides, too. This here is Mr. Gage Cameron. Opal is my wife, sir."

Gage touched his hat with a soft "Ma'am," studying the woman with a fascination he tried not to show.

She was nearly as tall as her husband, about twenty-five, and was almost pure black. Opal moved with a sinuous grace that was natural as sunrise, and her worn linsey dress didn't really disguise her lean, fine body. But her face was truly arresting. More handsome than beautiful, it was long, high-cheekboned, and almond-eyed. Grave, too, but with full lips that tipped up at the corners, just the trace of a smile. Gage was strongly reminded of a lithograph he'd once seen of the clay-molded bust of an ancient princess found in an Egyptian tomb. Except the princess

30

had been painted white or maybe tan-colored. But aside from the resemblance, this black woman's face held the same calm, half-aloof pride as that Egyptian lady's.

"Mr. Cameron . . . I thought you must be at least three men," she said. "Or are there others?"

"Just me," Gage said. "Those were RBJ men, as you folks may have known."

"Yeah," Reeve Bedoe said, swiping a trickle of blood from a cut on his broad brow. "Didn't 'dentify themselves none, but I figured."

Reeve made quite a study himself. His skin was darkly bronze, several shades lighter than his wife's, and he was built with the chunky, thick-bodied solidity of a young bull. He was in his early thirties. His eyes were large and quick; they hid nothing as they continued to assess Gage. Approving and yet cautious, as if wondering why this stranger had offered them such providential aid. His wide face with its squashed nose — as if it had been broken and healed crookedly — was far short of good-looking, but pleasant for all that. His sudden grin made it even more engaging.

"I sure am a mess," Reeve Bedoe said. "You're kind of banged up yourself."

"I reckon so."

"Well, you 'scuse me a minute, I'll clean up a mite."

Reeve tramped a few yards away to the water trough that stood downslope from a spring. A length of battered pipe fed fresh water into the trough; another pipe carried it out the other side. Reeve was a good man with his hands, from the snug, sound look of this place.

They were large, capable hands that now gingerly pulled off the remaining shreds of the shirt. His muscles writhed like fat snakes under his dusky bloodied skin as he splashed water over his head and trunk. He balled the remnants of cloth in a wad and began to sponge off his cuts, wincing and muttering under his breath. As the blood washed away Gage saw the crisscrossing of old scars on his back.

"You've been combed over before this, Mr. Bedoe." Gage said quietly, bluntly.

"Long spell back, sure." Reeve turned his head, grinning again. "Done some pretty fair mischief when I wasn't half-growed. Way 'fore Mr. Lincoln's proclamation and a couple more years 'fore the Yankee Army freed me. It wasn't no different afterward. Worse. Folks had to pay you then, and there wasn't no money to keep a poor freeman's belly filled. Got me out o' Georgia. Opal, she had it a sight easier, didn't you, honeybunch? Learned to talk fancy-fine 'n' all."

Opal smiled tranquilly, jiggling the now cooing baby in her arms. "Easier," she murmured ironically. "As body servant to the daughter of a rich man."

"Real soft livin', sure 'nough," Reeve said with his joshing grin.

"Yes," Opal Bedoe said tartly. "Private schooling, special tutoring. Taking in all I could while running errands for my mistress."

"Yeah, well," Reeve said tolerantly. "Don't you reckon that ought to count for somethin', Mr. Cameron?"

"It did," Opal said in her rich, modulated voice. "And a slave is still a slave." She turned her level gaze on Gage Cameron. "I was as destitute as any ex-slave when it was done. Reeve and I met in the Nations, later on. We were both working for a Cherokee family. I kept house on their ranch and Reeve helped herd sheep for them. Members of the so-called Five Civilized Tribes. They were about as civilized as any whites. They had kept slaves and had fought for the South."

Her tone held a hint of cool challenge, and Gage gave her one of his rare smiles.

"My folks were Navaho," he said. "They kept slaves at one time — other Indians. Go back far enough and just about any people you can name had slaves. The ones who could capture 'em. Or afford 'em."

Reeve shook the water from his kinky, close-cropped hair and came tramping back to them, still swabbing at his trunk. "Yeah, that's so. It don't give no answer to why you give us a hand, sir."

Briefly Gage told them how he had run afoul of the three riders, omitting any mention of his gold discovery. He concluded, "I was riding a grudge," then added, "and I'm not crazy about seeing anybody whipped."

"Well, that shines for certain." Reeve sighed grimly and looked off toward the swell of land where the RBJ men had vanished. "They be back sure."

"This is free grass," Gage said. "There's other homesteaders out and around. Or are you squatters?"

"Not squatters. Just niggers." Reeve spat sideways; the spittle was tinged with blood. "Bit my damn tongue. Ain't no others like us around. But I reckon they be out for any gov'ment 'steader pretty quick, that RBJ crowd. We was afeard it might come."

"You've settled kind of close to their line," Gage said. "Can't say just how close, but you must have known that much."

"Hell, we knowed. I got surprised. I was out workin' on them sheds and they come ridin' in here real easy, not a-sudden. They was even cordial, first off." Reeve shook his head. "Figured they just aimed to give me a hard talking-to. All at once they dabbed a couple ropes on me. Never looked for that. Here on, I keep my long gun near to hand."

Gage nodded. "It's as you said. They'll be back. The man who whipped you was Thad Overmile, old Janeece's nephew."

Reeve pursed his lips in a noiseless whistle. "They'll come a-steamin', then. But they'll come a heap more careful, after how you salted their tails. I be ready, too. Can't begin to thank you proper, but how would a cup o' coffee go? And

I sure wouldn't begrudge you a good snort o' whiskey. I got some."

"Thank you," Gage said gravely. "But you know what that stuff does to us Indians."

Reeve guffawed.

"Anyway," Gage added. "it's late in the day and I have to be getting home."

Opal asked, "Is your tribe nearby?"

Gage tipped his head toward the east. "Not too far. Those hills up next to the Neversummers. No tribe, though. Just a —" He checked himself. "I'll be going. Left my horse back on that rise."

"Listen," Reeve said. "Drop by again, will you, Mr. Cameron? We'll have that coffee or some firewater 'n' palaver some."

"I'll do that, Mr. Bedoe. When I have the time."

Reeve's ready grin flashed. "Just make it Reeve, would you? Ain't used to no misterin'."

"Neither am I. Make it Gage." He touched his hat to Opal, who smiled more fully now and said nothing. "Be seeing you both." He nodded solemnly at the baby. "You, too."

CHAPTER FOUR

For a while Gage had nearly forgotten the drag of weariness in his bruised body. Because he was dead tired now, all the brutal aches sank back into his muscles with a monotonous throbbing.

He came off the undulating flats east of Reeve Bedoe's homestead claim into the steadily inclining uplands that marked the foothills below the western slopes of the Neversummer Mountains. He rode more slowly now because the pink-yellow daylight had flattened along the horizon at his back, gold sunset blurring into pearly twilight.

For almost an hour he was able to follow the winding course of the Los Pinos where it made a deep northeasterly bend, then swung due north again. It trickled narrowly down out of the high peaks until, fed by excessive meltwater from the spring thaws, it would gather strength for a descent into the boiling rapids below.

Gage cut away from the riverbank well before he came to that last northern crook of the river. He rode into dense stands of lofty pines that stood blackly serrated against the twilight sky, ranging easily through the crowding timber along old game and Indian trails that he knew as well as he knew the seams of his palms. As the last light

36

ebbed into dusk, then into near-total darkness, he picked his way even more slowly but still confidently among the trees, feeling the strong upland swell of land beneath his horse.

Tiredly Gage reviewed the afternoon's events in his mind. He knew a few things he must do for sure. One was to have the line between RBJ's patented land and the public domain grass properly surveyed — on the quiet. Generally the Los Pinos was regarded as the natural boundary between RBJ and the open range to the east and Mungo Cameron's high country holdings to the north.

If it really was, then his gold find lay within the public domain still open to federal homesteaders. Legally, at least, Gage could stake a claim there without running afoul of the law. But he couldn't file it at the U. S. Land Office in Glade without risking the revelation of what he wanted to keep hushed up. Any person who, on purpose or on idle whim, cared to examine the claim-register charts had a right to do so.

If interested parties were then curious enough to investigate why Gage Cameron had filed a claim at that particular place when his family's holdings lay well to the northeast, they might comb the ground and learn the reason. He couldn't keep constant guard over the area, not if he was to dig any more gold out in secrecy. Working in the open on that precarious escarpment would be difficult at best, damned dangerous at worst. He'd be in danger from claim jumpers of every stripe, who, watching their chance, might take him by surprise.

Was he being overly cautious? After all that had happened in a single afternoon, Gage didn't believe he could be too wary. Or too edgy.

Even in his fog of weariness, memory of the sighing coldness that had swept him at the deserted Navaho camp still quilled his skin with gooseflesh. He had to resolve that ominous portent in his own mind before he proceeded further. He knew only one possible way. His venerable kinsman Adakhai was versed in the age-old lore of the Dineh. As much as he detested the idea of giving the aged shaman the satisfaction of consulting his advice, Gage resignedly decided he had no choice.

The pine-bound blackness around him conveyed no threat to his trained senses. Any menace that might lurk in it wouldn't be supernatural. Baked out by sun warmth, the strong odor of pine resin still held pleasant in the cooling air. Somewhere overhead a great horned owl hooted and then flew, coasting unseen in the night. The roan gelding found its way surefootedly along the dark, twisting trails that it knew by instinct and familiarity as well as its master did.

All Gage Cameron's boyhood had been spent in this country, broken only by a four-year exile to the Indian school at Carlisle, Pennsylvania. He had hated that interlude with a silent passion. The repression of his Indian half, the stifling of his freeborn nature. When he'd returned to the

West and his familiar stamping grounds, it had been for good.

Some men needed the wine of freedom as much as others needed whiskey or opium. Gage was one of them. Yet his schooling at Carlisle had left him firmly, if cynically, grounded in the white man's ways, which his always-curious mind had absorbed like a sponge. It had also tinged the bedrock of his freewheeling nature with a sense of personal responsibility that held more of a white man's familial feeling than an Indian's tribal or clan allegiance.

You're a cross-dog mixture, all right, he thought. But maybe you can make it work for you and yours . . . at last. Properly handled, the gold would be the key to what so far had eluded his ambitions for the Camerons.

The pines thinned away into isolated trees that dotted a wide clearing. Ahead were the lit windows of the Cameron dwelling. Gage's eyes swam with a slow stupor of exhaustion; the windows were no more than squared yellow blurs in his vision. Beyond the black, low block of the small house were a few log outsheds, dark, deserted, and unseen. One of them housed the three men who herded the outfit's sheep, but all of them would be out on-range tonight.

Old Tobe, the family dog, picked up the scent of horse and man and came off the porch yapping. He quit immediately at Gage's mild "Shut up" as he rode forward into the rectangles of window-flung lamplight.

Gage halted his horse in the yard, then just sat his saddle a moment, not trusting himself to dismount at once without falling on his face. Setting his teeth against a multitude of aches, he swung to the ground. Tobe capered around horse and man, tail wagging wildly. Standing stiff-legged, one arm flung across his saddle, Gage rubbed the big hound's head for a full minute, speaking silly lingo to him. Afterward he tied his reins to a porch post and mechanically slid his Winchester from its scabbard before tramping drag-footed across the porch. He opened the door and drew it shut behind him as he stepped inside.

His father was slumped on one side of two benches flanking the puncheon table that centered the room. His brother was seated by a wall with his crossed legs straight out in front of him, cleaning his rifle with an oily rag. His sister was washing dishes at a half-log counter by the opposite wall. None of them was exchanging any conversation, and none bothered to glance at Gage as he entered.

Business as usual, he thought sourly.

The room was fairly spacious, and the lamp on the middle of the table shed a mellow and falsely welcoming glow over log walls adorned with a few faded lithograph prints. To one side and to the rear were four doorways covered with jute-sack curtains; each person had a separate bedroom and, being the chummy lot they were, wouldn't have had it any other way.

Without looking around, Amber said, "We ate

40

an hour ago. You fetched any rabbits, you gut and skin 'em yourself."

Gage said, "I didn't," as he gingerly eased onto the bench across from the old man and leaned his rifle against it. "Anything left from supper?"

"It's cold," Amber said.

"That's all right. Just heat the coffee."

Ran said, grinning, "No nail-'em rabbit, uh, Chief? Bagged three today my own self."

"Good for you."

Ran glanced up now, his eyes widening at first sight of his brother's scabbed face. "Holy cow. Who made your handsome puss over?"

Mungo Cameron raised his shaggy head, staring owlishly, and Amber swung around, holding a soapy dish. "Criminies," she murmured. "You're dirtier'n a pile a shitty diapers, Gage."

"*Used* diapers," Mungo rumbled in a kind of reflex reprimand. "How many times you been told to watch your mouth, lassie?"

"I lost count ten years ago."

"Aye. Maybe washing it out with a pannikin o' that soapy water would cleanse it?"

"Want to try it?" Amber invited, setting a fist on her hip. "You'd have to get on your feet first, though. Other hand, booze might be better. Sure has cleaned your old clock proper, ain't it, Pappy?"

Gage was too accustomed to the unguardedly snotty banter that ordinarily prevailed in this household to pay much attention to it.

Mungo only grunted disinterestedly, dropping

his gaze back to the tin cup cradled between his huge hands. He swallowed the remaining contents and reached for the jug at his elbow. After supper, he usually got drunker than he was most of the day.

Mungo Cameron was a stocky block of a man who wasn't quite sixty and looked seventy. He had a full head of bushy hair, but it bore only a few streaks of its former flaming red, now gone to a dull brick color. It wasn't nearly as ruddy as his broad and bloated face, pouched around bloodshot eyes that had once been fiercely alert blue. Gage had inherited his thick wedge of a nose, minus its whiskey-veined redness. Mungo's massive shoulders sagged toward a barrel chest, which in time had mostly collapsed into his belly.

Amber dried her hands on a piece of frayed calico and went to the fieldstone fireplace. She hung the big cow-camp coffeepot on an iron trammel over the glowing coals and slapped a cold steak and some chunks of corn bread on a platter.

"Come on," Ran said with sly but curious amusement. "How you get all banged up that way? You tangle with a rabbit and he was too feisty for you?"

"That's right," Gage said. "Dabbed my lasso on one and he dragged me on my face a half mile."

"Couldn't do it much harm at that," Ran observed. "But sounds like big poop, Chief."

"It's enough for you. My horse is tied outside.

Put him up. Walk him for a spell, then water and grain him."

"Why?"

Ran grinned insolently. He was eighteen, about Gage's size and heft and, like his older brother, was as quick and flexible as a twist of seasoned whip leather.

"I'm too beat up to do it, that's why."

"Pretty horseshit reason."

"Sometimes," Gage said quietly, "you seem to have pure diarrhea of the mouth, sonny. Tonight isn't a good time for it."

"Yeah?" The familiar mocking lights kindled in Ran's black eyes. "You'd have to prove it, and you ain't in no shape to."

"I will be. Day or so of rest and I'll be able to beat the living daylights out of you. How's that for a reason?"

Ran eyed him carefully. He could see Gage meant it, and they had tangled before. Gage, ten years his elder, could still lay Ran's lithe but only half-coordinated frame in the dust with comparative ease. Ran was badly tempted, even so, and was confident the day would come when he could outmatch his brother.

"Think ahead," Gage murmured.

"Hell, I am." Ran grinned, unfazed. "More ways than one. Someday it'll be *your* sweet ass gets dumped, Chief."

"I can hardly wait, Randolph," Gage said tolerantly, just watching him.

Ran laughed suddenly, even good-naturedly.

He laid aside the rifle, lunged to his feet, and slouched out the door, still chuckling.

He and Gage were much alike in their love of hunting and woods roving but got along so badly that they rarely pursued their interests in company. The kid's a burr under my saddle, Gage thought bleakly. Always was. Have to try to get over that. Get through to him somehow, dammit.

Reaching across the table, he scooped up his father's jug on a forefinger, hoisted it over to his nose, and sniffed the mouth. The flat, strong pungence of a Navaho brew rose from it.

Instantly Mungo bristled: his bloodshot eyes lit as fiercely blue as they'd ever been. "Be handing that back laddie. Now!"

Gage said, "Just curious. *Toghlepai,* eh? No need to ask. You ran out of whiskey. Again."

Mungo reached out and snatched the jug, nearly dislocating Gage's finger. "Dinna ye ever touch my nerve tonic again! Aye, at least I got some thoughtful kin will fetch me a draught when no ungrateful damned whelps o' mine will!"

He poured another whopping cupful, grumbling about his born offspring's damnable ingratitude. Amber carried a steaming cup of coffee and the platter of steak and bread to the table, setting them in front of Gage. She was smiling a little, showing her fine white teeth.

"*Tonic.* Poison is more like."

"Shut your bleedin' ungrateful mouth, wench!"

Amber made a face at her father and went back

to the dishpan, loudly clattering the dishes in it.

She was seventeen and small, graceful as a young willow, trim and tawny-skinned and undeniably lovely. Her hair, black and shiny as a crow's wing, matched her intense and sparkling eyes. The hem of her thin cotton dress ended at the calves, like a Mexican girl's, more than hinting at the slim-legged beauty above. Her daintily formed feet were bare, and over a long period they had worn mildly hollowed paths on the hard-packed clay floor where she walked most often during a day's housekeeping.

For Amber was diligent enough. No denying that, even if Gage deplored her sometimes wanton ways away from home. He knew from plentiful if scattered hearsay that she was a merciless tease among the Navaho lads here on the plateau. Not that there were many to worry about, and he was just grateful that she hadn't (as far as he knew) plied her wiles with any young white men. That could land her, and all of them, in real trouble.

In their immediate family, only Amber and Ran sometimes got along amiably. Why not? Both were natural troublemakers, ready for any kind of hell-raising frolic they fancied they could get away with. Practically birds of a feather, even to closely resembling each other. Both were handsome by white standards, slim-faced with narrow, sculpted features. Unlike Gage himself, who might have been facially modeled after his father (close to downright ugly), though Indian-looking in every other way, Amber and Ran took after their mother, Morning Light, an attractive woman by the ideals of any race.

No doubt that fact had first seized Mungo Cameron's interest thirty years ago when, as a lone Scottish immigrant, footloose and roaming, he had met Morning Light in Canyon de Chelly, the old Navaho stronghold. Mungo had swifty wooed and won the fifteen-year-old girl, and theirs had been a long and loving union.

Gage had been their first child, and Morning Light had borne three more children after him, all of them dying in infancy. Then had come Ran and Amber. Morning Light herself had died while bearing a final stillborn child.

Soon after that, a dozen years before, Mungo Cameron had settled into a daily ritual of steady drinking. His tragedy had been that he'd come to love one woman too much. His boozing had never stopped; it had grown steadily worse over the years.

Ran came back inside and slacked into his chair. "Okay, Chief. Your nag is put up all nice and cozy. Anything else?"

Gage was eating his meal with no real appetite, sunk in his morose thoughts. He merely shook his head.

Finished, he rose and carried the utensils over to Amber, who gave him a curious look. "Something fretting you, Gage?"

"Off my feed, I reckon. Took a spill from my horse today."

"Oh, that all it was? How you got all marked up?"

Anytime Amber or Ran showed a trace of concern, they quickly managed to nullify it. Still, it lent Gage hope that he might harness their young energies in a useful direction. Neither had ever shown any intellectual curiosity — no white person's schooling for them — yet both were as quick-witted as they were full of sass.

Not replying, Gage moved over to the big, crudely made bookcase set against one wall. It was packed with well-thumbed books of all kinds: scientific works, collections of belles lettres, and some works of fiction, mostly by Jane Austen and Charles Dickens. At one time Mungo had been an avid reader, and Gage had read all of Mungo's books and had added some of his own to the library.

Gage slipped Bernewitz's *Book for Prospectors* from the bottom shelf, holding the cover against his leg sort of covertly as he went to his room and drew the jute-sack drape for privacy. That alone wouldn't arouse anyone's curiosity; Gage had always been in the habit of reading for a while before he went to sleep.

The room was hardly large enough to contain his narrow bunk and a bedside stand with a lamp on it. Gage lit the lamp, turned the flame low, and dug the nugget samples out of his pocket before settling onto his corn-shuck-filled pallet with a groan of relief. He'd never wanted more to drop immediately off to sleep, but his ferment of excited discovery was still high.

He thumbed through Bernewitz's slim volume, looking for tests by which to determine whether a piece of ore was worthless or the real stuff. If it couldn't be scratched with a knife, it wasn't pyrite; if it crumbled to powder under the knife, it wasn't pyrrhotite; if it could be beaten into malleable contortions without breaking, it wasn't chalcopyrite.

He turned the nuggets over and over in his fingers, studying their glittering facets, and decided he wouldn't chance arousing any attention by testing the stuff right now. Yawning, he blew out the lamp and shoved the samples under the folded horse blanket that served as his pillow.

Tomorrow . . . first thing.

Even as the thought formed, his eyes closed. He fell into a deep, undreaming sleep with the open book propped facedown on his belly.

CHAPTER FIVE

Thad was roused by Carmen Paz firmly knocking on his door and saying briskly, "Senor! Up, now. Your uncle is home. He wan' talk to you."

Thad tried to burrow farther into his blankets, wincing at the deep ache that shot up his right leg. The pain had caused him to sleep fitfully for hours before falling into a sweaty slumber. He blinked sluggishly, his eyelids feeling as if they were coated with glue, and mumbled, "Wha'?"

"Your uncle arrive home late las' night," Carmen said. "Now he is at breakfast. He wan' talk to you, he say. I was you, senor, I wouldn' keep him waiting none."

"Christ," Thad groaned.

"*¿Qué?*"

"*Jesús*, if that suits you better. All right. Tell his lordship to keep his hunting shirt on. I'll be there directly."

The housekeeper's steps made a brisk rapping as she walked away down the corridor. Thad threw aside the blankets and rolled heavily off the bed, sitting on its edge a moment, scratching one bare thigh and running his hands through his rumpled hair before he rose to his feet. He cursed thinly as he limped over to the full-length mirror and inspected his tall, naked body.

Thaddeus Overmile rarely greeted the dawn in a sweet frame of mind and was particularly surly this morning, silently raging at the unknown bastard who'd shot away his boot heel yesterday. The impact of the bullet that had twisted his legs in midrun had resulted in a badly wrenched muscle in his right calf. It had remained sore as hell afterward and of course was stiff as hell this morning. It would be a while working out its kinks.

Even the sight of his well-built body in the mirror, his long, arrogantly handsome face with its crown of light, wavy hair, failed to improve Thad's mood. He was in the superbly robust condition of a man in his prime, just topping thirty; seeing himself full-length each morning usually gave him a needed lift of pleasure. But not today. His hurt calf was swollen and bore a deep purplish bruise.

Thad hobbled over to his commode and got out a clean change of clothes, ignoring the dirty duds he had chucked carelessly in a corner when retiring early last night. He'd felt lousy enough to oversleep and wanted to sleep some more, but whenever Uncle Robert said "frog," you'd best jump. That's if he aimed to go on holding down the fine, cozy berth he occupied at RBJ because of Uncle's largess.

The linsey curtains on the single west-facing window of his room, bellied on a fresh morning breeze, promised another warm and pleasant day in the Wyoming high country. It carried the faint drone of Hurd Tancred's voice upslope from the corrals where the RBJ crewmen were assembled, getting their day's orders.

That goddamned son of a bitch, Thad thought with a customary vicious reflex.

He didn't have to make out Hurd's speech; just the sound of his flat and imperturbable voice was enough to draw Thad's nerves on edge. He and the RBJ foreman had never gotten along, and he knew it would be worse after yesterday.

Thad slid into his fresh underwear and change of tailored well-cut pants and shirt, and then — forgoing his usual varied taste in fancy footwear — selected a pair of run-over boots that had once been costly Justins. Now they were old and soft-worn, but they had both heels intact and were easier to work onto his feet than any of his newer, stiffer boots. Nevertheless, wrestling on the right boot, he still swore feelingly at the pain that shot through his calf. Afterward he combed his hair before the mirror, carefully parting it, and wondered if he could spare the time to shave. Better not. Not with R. B. waiting to have palaver with him.

That goddamned Hurd, he thought again savagely. Sure as hell those two guys, or one of 'em, spilled the beans to the whole crew, and I'll lay odds he heard it and told R. B.

Thad shrugged into his expensive jacket, finely cured buckskin with a dripping of fringes along the sleeves, and gazed at his reflection with moderate satisfaction and no less than his usual vanity. Afterward he left his room and limped down the corridor to the main section of the house.

It was a long, one-story building set on a slight elevation above the sprawl of outbuildings and tangle of corrals. The house and all the outsheds were fashioned entirely of massive squared pine logs, for the original owner had taken the pains to build for solidity and permanence. The central part of the ranch house consisted of two parlors and a dining room, with two flanking wings. The east one contained a pantry and kitchen and storage facilities. The west wing, from which Thad now emerged, had six bedrooms opening onto a central hallway.

Thad's nose wrinkled with his usual distaste as he stepped into the rear parlor. The annoying whiff of animal musk repelled him as much as ever. It exuded from the trophy heads that decorated all the inside walls of the front and back parlors and the dining room, to the exclusion of nearly anything else.

Goddamn R. B. and his insatiable lust for hunting.

Not that Thad had any ethical objections to the sport; he'd occasionally enjoyed it himself. Most men did. But Uncle Robert's interest ran far beyond a mere passion or obsession. R. B. Janeece had used his inherited fortune to roam the entire globe, killing all manner of big game and preserving only the biggest and best heads as trophy specimens.

Heads of animals from every continent dominated the walls. R. B. wasn't ordinarily much of a conversationalist, but he would wax enthusiastically on his trophies; he could name each species and where he had bagged it. He didn't even care whether you were listening to him or not. Thad had often been his reluctant listener and thus had soaked up a lot of big-game hunting lore himself, though he still couldn't identify all the many species.

Scattered in no particular order throughout the rooms were the heads of big carnivorous cats (Uncle Robert's favorite kills), including African lions and leopards and cheetahs, mountain lions and jaguars. Tibetan snow leopards, Asian clouded leopards. Also quite a few canine specimens: African hyena and aardwolf, Norwegian blue fox, black fox, and Canadian timber wolf.

Gathered from around the world were heads of North American elk, white-tailed and mule deer and pronghorn antelope, ibex, chamois, and a variety of African antelope: impala, kudu, hartebeest, waterbuck, wildebeest, klipspringer, several kinds of gazelle, and a giant eland. There was a single kangaroo-head trophy and two massive bull elephant heads, one African and one Indian, complete with tusks.

R. B. had taken American black bear, a polar bear, a Himalayan sun bear, and a huge Chinese panda. There were heads of an Arctic musk-ox and an American bison, and several of the heavily horned Cape buffalo of South Africa, which Uncle Robert averred was the most dangerous animal on earth. Privately Thad had long concluded that it ran a poor second to Uncle Robert himself.

R. B. had one quirk — he never shot birds. He claimed he admired their free-soaring freedom too much. And fishing was only a minor sideline of his, although he had one wall crowded with beautifully mounted specimens of swordfish, tarpon, striped marlin, black marlin, tuna, barracuda, mako sharks, and sturgeon along with the more prosaic American inland fish, such as muskellunge and northern pike.

There was also a plentiful scattering of heterogeneous pelt rugs on the stone floors. Thad hobbled across them to reach the dining room doorway off the front parlor.

The dining area was large and roomy. It contained a huge fieldstone fireplace and a long oak table with four matched, carved armchairs on either side, plus single chairs placed at the head and foot. Old Hermann Gottlieb, the previous owner, had entertained guests lavishly and often. R. B. never entertained, but perversely he liked to keep up appearances. He always occupied the head chair at the table, and Thad would diplomatically seat himself at its foot.

Like the two parlors, the dining room walls held only game heads, except for the glass, walnut-framed gun case at R. B.'s back. It was fully twelve feet wide and contained an incredible array of hard-hitting armament. Rifles of every kind imported from all over Europe, as well as American Colt revolvers, up-to-date Henrys and Winchesters, old-time muskets, and Kentucky long rifles, kept for show only. But Uncle Robert's favorite weapons were the powerful Martini express rifles of British make; he had four of them on display.

"Morning, Uncle Bob." Thad gave R. B. a polite nod as he seated himself at his usual place.

"Morning, Thad . . . good morning!"

R. B. sounded affable enough, but that didn't mean a damned lot, Thad had learned. His avuncular relative could greet you in a tone as smooth as cream, then suddenly drop a crusher.

R. B. Janeece was a rather short man, trim and wiry, his slight frame packed with nervous strength and energy. He had a full thatch of pure white hair and a weather-lined ruddily brown face bisected by a neatly clipped steer-horn mustache. Thad wasn't sure of his exact age but thought it was somewhere in the early fifties. R. B. was dressed in his usual fashion, managing to look dapper and immaculate in tan canvas hunting togs that he ordered directly from Levi Strauss, having them cut and made to his own specifications. After he went on a hunting expedition, his previous set of clothing would be torn and soiled. That was nothing to R. B.; he'd simply replace it with a new and identical outfit.

"Well" — R. B. flashed his big square teeth in a smile — "how have things been during my absence, Thaddeus?"

"Oh, *poco a poco,* I guess," Thad said carefully.

"You're limping. And your face seems a bit roughed up."

"Yeah, I guess it is. How did your hunt go?"

"Splendidly! Splendidly, my boy . . ."

R. B. ran on at considerable length about the success of his just-finished foray. He and Patchy had ranged far afield into the Neversummer peaks, hoping to bring down a North American grizzly. Oddly, in all his years of hunting, R. B. had never even glimpsed a grizzly bear, let alone shot one. This time he'd been lucky. The huge grizzly had been a fierce and frightening spectacle as it charged R. B. after his first shot hadn't proved fatal. His second bullet had brought it crashing to the ground.

"Must weigh out well over a thousand pounds. Best damned kill of my life, after the Cape buffalo." R. B. smiled contentedly.

He snapped his fingers. "Mrs. Paz! Bring in our young man's breakfast. And more coffee for me, please."

After a few moments Carmen entered from the adjoining kitchen, deftly bumping open the swing door with her hip, and carried a tray to the table. She filled R. B.'s cup from a steaming pitcher, then set Thad's breakfast in front of him — a big platter of ham and eggs and hot flapjacks, and a cup of coffee.

Thad attacked his food hungrily, at the same time sneaking appreciative glances at Carmen Paz.

Dressed neatly in a black maid's uniform, with a frill of white lace on her smooth black hair, she was olive-skinned with an oval, high-boned face. About thirty-five, she must have been a beauty in her younger days. She still was, for that matter, though somewhat on the buxom side. Carmen was the wife of Chino Paz, the horse wrangler for RBJ; the two shared a comfortable log cabin nearby. She was R. B.'s full-time housekeeper, and she kept his trophy-ridden house spanking clean.

Yes sir, quite a woman. Thad envied Chino Paz but was too shrewd to make a move for Carmen. She was too briskly matter-of-fact to be easily taken in by any smart-talking gringo. But Thad had a tremendous sweet tooth for good-looking, dark-skinned gals. Such as Amber Cameron. God, but he'd like to make it with her. And that nigger Reeve Bedoe's tall black wife. Man, she was really something. . . .

Somebody knocked on the outside door that opened into the dining room.

"Come in, Hurd," R. B. said in a jovial voice.

Thad had been expecting as much. Hurd Tancred entered, pulling off his battered hat.

"Sit down, Hurd," R. B. said. "Have something to eat?"

"Thanks all the same. Already ate at the cook-shack with the boys, Mr. Janeece."

"Have a cup of coffee anyway."

The chair groaned under Hurd's weight as he settled onto it, halfway between R. B. and Thad.

He was being semi-deferential to his employer, not at all to his employer's nephew. Hurd gave Carmen a brief nod of thanks as she set a cup in front of him.

Hurd Tancred was about forty, built as broad as a hogshead in his worn and shapeless range clothes, and if you could call him fat, it was damned hard fat. His head sat on his body like a square block, almost neckless, and his scanty saddle of roan hair was cropped close to his scalp. Hurd's thick face was stolid and expressionless; he looked anything but intelligent, but he was. He was damned intelligent.

Some seven years before, after R. B. had paid out a huge sum to obtain this ranch, he had given Hurd the entire responsibility of running it, from giving the crew hands all their orders to keeping tally on the ranch books. The man's past was a mystery. Thad had no idea how or where R. B. had first gotten in contact with Hurd.

And Hurd had made the once-declining outfit prosper; Thad had to give the bastard credit for that. R. B. had absolute confidence in him, and for good reason. Hurd received a huge salary and a cut of the annual profits, and he worked hard to earn them, wholly freeing R. B. Janeece for his lifelong absorption in hunting. R. B. couldn't have maintained his own ongoing costly pursuit without the income provided by Hurd's competent maintenance of the RBJ spread. Ranching was as much in Hurd Tancred's blood as hunting was in R. B.'s.

"Well, gentlemen." R. B. Janeece smiled genially, leaning back in his chair. "Thaddeus . . . last night when I got in, Hurd apprised me of your little venture over on the public-domain grass. Undertaken without my knowledge. Eh?"

Thad chewed a piece of ham and swallowed it, and only then he looked up from his plate. "It was just that one nigger, Uncle Bob. Didn't figure you'd object —"

"To putting one darky in his place? Certainly not," Janeece said crisply. "But the fellow is not a squatter, Thad. His portion is staked out as a government homestead, legitimately registered at the U. S. Land Office. So Hurd has told me. You weren't aware of *that?*"

"Oh . . . sure." Thad cleared his throat, finding his appetite gone. Uncle Robert wasn't idly disputing the matter; the glint in his metal blue eyes showed a cold displeasure. "Happens I checked at the land office while you were away."

"Splendid. So then you made the move on your own, without consulting me. And without asking Hurd's advice."

Thad took a sip of his coffee. He was careful not to look at Hurd Tancred, who wouldn't show a trace of emotion anyway.

"Well, yeah. Look, Uncle Bob. Before a 'steader can claim that a hundred and sixty acres are his, he has to live on it for six months' time. Right?"

"So?"

"We just aimed to hustle this bugger's black ass off his claim soon as we could. If he quits

59

it before it becomes his, it's not his, right?"

Janeece slapped one hand on the table with a flat, hard impact that nearly caused Thad to spill his coffee. "Of course not! But other federal homesteaders have settled on the public-domain lands west of our boundary. You knew that!"

"Well, you never tried to stop 'em, sir," Thad said blandly. "But you've objected often enough to what they're doing."

"Yes! Because they are gradually absorbing open range, where this outfit has freely grazed its stock since time out of mind." R. B. Janeece's gaze was still flicking blue lights as it shuttled to Hurd Tancred. "Is that right, Hurd?"

"Right as rain, sir."

Tancred's wide, sleepy face wore its usual casually indifferent look as he reached across the table to a glass that held a bunch of toothpicks. He stuck one in the corner of his mouth and only then glanced at Thad. He didn't smile and didn't have to. Thad could sense the smug amusement under the bastard's face without having to guess.

"Another thing," R. B. continued relentlessly. "I understand you gave that darky a whipping, only to be driven off by some people firing on you from the heights. Jesus, boy, but that was stupid! Getting yourself into a bind like that!"

Thad shot Hurd a brief venomous glance.

He'd taken two men with him on the mission — a simple-minded puncher named Tuck Cotter and a quietly sinister man known only as Breck.

Both were RBJ crewmen who would do whatever they were bidden. Tuck, because he was acquiescent to any suggestion and also plain damned dumb. Breck, because he was by profession a cold-blooded troubleshooter, a bravo who was kept on the crew at a top hand's wage in case of trouble that could be handled only in a pushy extreme. He could be relied on to keep his mouth shut unless queried directly.

So it must have been Tuck Cotter who had blabbed about the matter to other members of the crew (although Thad had warned him not to), and word must have circulated back to Tancred almost at once. Hurd would have promptly questioned Breck also and then conveyed the information directly back to R. B. Janeece immediately after his return last night.

This was a moment to back and fill, Thad knew warily. "You're right, Uncle Bob," he said humbly. "But I still can't figure how the hell it happened. How could that nigger be cagey enough to know we were coming to his place? Even if he was, where did he get all those men to lay up for him?"

"Could be he didn't," Hurd Tancred observed in his soft, sleepy way, shifting the toothpick from one side of his mouth to the other. "What I heard, you boys had done some shooting at that breed Gage Cameron. He fell off a slope 'longside the Los Pinos and you shot all 'round him whilst he was hanging there by an eyelash. Could be he trailed you up later and done some smokin'

61

right back at you."

"Bullshit!" Thad said hotly. "There must have been three or four guys shooting at us from up there —"

"That'll do," Janeece put in icily. "Whatever the situation was, Thad, you not only failed in your intent, you've made RBJ and all of us look like fools. Word is bound to get around; it always does. How can you keep men from talking, even men on your own crew? I could forgive your indiscretion or even your asininity. But not that."

Thad felt a flush of heat crawl from his neck up to his face. But he looked down at his plate and said contritely, "Right again, Uncle Bob. I just wasn't thinking far enough ahead."

"True. But you'd better get in the habit." R. B. spoke quietly but with a hint of acid contempt. "I've always been indulgent to a fault with you because of a promise I made your mother on her deathbed — to take your upbringing in hand, raise you the best way I could. I've tried to. I've paid off your various gambling debts, and twice I've bailed you out of trouble with women. It was my money that turned the trick. And don't you by God forget it."

But as a father, or even as a halfway decent uncle, you aren't worth a shit, Thad thought in a rare moment of insight. You saw I got a good education, but when did I ever get anything more from you? A kid might as well try to be close to a piece of rock.

Out loud he said only, "I haven't forgotten it, sir."

"Then show it to better effect, eh?" Janeece shifted his weight forward, tapping a forefinger on the table. "Perhaps I failed to make myself clear before, but I won't now. I know you aspire to be a working part of our operation here. Excellent. I approve. But when I am not here, you'll defer *strictly* to Hurd's orders. Make no bright move of your own without consulting him first. He knows my wishes as to any decision affecting the outfit and how it's to be carried out. Understood?"

"Yes, sir." Thad's face was still burning, and he had to clench both hands in his lap to hide their trembling.

His hatred of Hurd Tancred had deepened by another notch. Some rancor now extended to his uncle as well. R. B. had bawled him out before, but there'd been no call for him to scold him like a wet-eared kid in front of Hurd. Goddamn them both.

Hurd Tancred cleared his throat mildly. "Thad might be partly right, though, Mr. Janeece."

"How's that, Hurd?"

"Well . . ." Hurd took the soggy toothpick from his lips and dropped it into his coffee cup. "I never put forward a whole lot of suggestions on how the outfit should be run. Just managed things according to how you want, with your best interests in mind."

"That's true, and I've appreciated it. But don't

63

be coy now, Hurd. If you have something to say, I'd like to hear it straight out."

Hurd nodded. "You said it yourself and I agreed. Them federal 'steaders been eating into the open graze. Not much so far, but they'll be crowding in like wildfire in a few years. It's going to cost us dear in the long run."

"Hardly any question about that." R. B. brushed a finger across his white-saber mustache. "But I won't go against the law, Hurd. You know that. It would hurt even worse in the long run."

Tancred waggled his heavy block of a head. "I know what you're *saying,* sir. And I don't want to talk out of turn —"

"Damn it, man, be forthright. What are you getting at?"

"That what's concerning you ain't the legality of matters," Hurd said quietly, bluntly. "It's what you, or we, can get away with. Legally or not."

Hurd calmly plucked another toothpick from the glass and inserted it into his mouth, his indifferent gaze locking with R. B.'s chilly one.

Thad felt a sudden and surprised lift at Tancred's words. Usually a man could hardly guess what was on Hurd's mind. Wisely Thad said nothing. He was fairly sure of just how amoral and ruthless R. B. could be if you gave him a comfortable margin of safety.

"Why, that's true, of course," Janeece said slowly. "Do you have any further 'suggestions'?"

"A few."

"Then carry on."

"Maybe you'd prefer that I leave the room," Thad said in a tone of wholly spurious humility.

"Balderdash, my boy." Janeece had made his point; he could afford to lavish a large and generous smile on his nephew. "Stay, by all means. We might both learn something. Go on, Hurd."

"That nigger Bedoe's claim is far and away the closest to our boundary line. Thad was right if his thinkin' was if he put the run on him, we could fetch the other 'steaders a lesson they won't forget. It's worked in other places I know of."

Both men glanced at Thad, who only inclined his head in a mock-humble assent.

"There's ways," Tancred went on, "that ain't legal by no means. But none of 'em would involve any legal risk to us."

For nearly a half hour Hurd talked quietly and confidently, underpitching his voice so his words wouldn't reach Carmen in the kitchen. The three men let their coffee go cold and the grease marble on their plates. Thad had never heard a fraction of this much talk out of Tancred at any time. But, obviously, it had been on his mind for some while.

R. B. broke in only from time to time, asking for clarification on a few points.

Finally Hurd said tranquilly, "That's about it, Mr. Janeece. Them's the different ways we can move this nigger off and not get our butts in a squeeze. If one way don't work, might be another one will."

"Very good, Hurd. Good." R. B. steepled his fingers together under his face, smiling. "Afraid I won't be around to see it happen. Patchy and I will be setting off on another hunt tomorrow. I've learned of another grizzly bear, far bigger even than the one I've bagged, up in the same mountain area. Gigantic devil, in his prime, and a real menace to the few settlers up in those peaks. Seems he's killed a lot of their livestock. By Gadfrey, I want to dust this fellow off myself."

"You can trust me." Hurd said.

"I'm sure. And I want to trust Thad as well. He's hardly stupid. But still somewhat young, headstrong, and impulsive at times. And spoiled. God knows, but I suppose that was my own doing. He'll come around in time, I'm sure. Meantime he'll be under your absolute orders."

Thad nodded. "That's already understood, Uncle Bob."

"Then let's adjourn this caucus for now." Janeece patted his lips with his napkin, scraped back his chair, and stood up. "I want to get my gear in order. Patchy and I will be leaving first thing tomorrow. We three will get together again here for supper. Meantime the two of you put your heads together and see if you can come up with any useful . . . elaborations."

Just that peremptorily, both men were dismissed. R. B. wanted no more to do with ranch

66

problems than he had to, aside from keeping apprised of them. He was already preoccupied with his next hunting foray.

CHAPTER SIX

Hurd Tancred clamped on his hat and tramped out the door, his bulk swaying from side to side in the way of any massively built man. Thad followed and fell into step beside him as they headed in the general direction of the corrals. Thad's unabated hatred for the foreman was still riding a high, hot edge.

"Well, nephew," Hurd said, not looking at him. "You want to palaver now?"

"Sure," Thad said thinly, coming to a halt. "I want to get something settled with you, pigface. Now's as good a time as any."

Hurd came to a stop, too. He spit the toothpick to the ground between them. It landed an inch from Thad's right boot. "Uh-huh, yeah. You aim to dispute what your uncle swore you on? Wouldn't be no way judicious, sonny."

"No," Thad agreed. "That would be dumb, which I'm not. Neither are you. I agree with the suggestions you made, pigface. Sounded fine. We can work together. You're aware that I'm Uncle Robert's sole heir to his property and money. I've seen his will. And just now, he didn't remotely indicate that he intended to change it any."

"Yeah," Tancred said with the faintest hint of a smile. "I seen that will, too. I got no say-so in the matter, boyo. But you'd best toe the line with me after today."

"I will. And you might just be out of a nice, comfy position on the day I take over this outfit."

Hurd grunted. "Suits me. I don't reckon you 'n' me will ever rub each other any way 'cept against the bristles. But I got a feeling the old man might be good for another twenty or so years yet. He's got a mighty hazardous hobby, or occupation, whatever it is. But he ain't no fool either, and he ain't lived this long and nary a scratch on his carcass if he was."

Hurd paused, rumbling a deep, toneless chuckle. "Twenty or so years, you philanderin' little turd? Why, I'll be set for pasture myself by then. I aim to live out my remaining time in rich fettle. I sure as hell don't aim to spend it cleaning up your piddle soon as you start makin' a mess o' things. You will."

Thad was pleased. He liked having the issue out in the open. He even liked Hurd's taunting epithet. It helped define their mutual hatred. Thad wasn't little; he stood inches taller than Hurd Tancred and was years younger, and he was in excellent condition himself.

"Good," he muttered. "That's good, piggy. You oink-oink exactly as I'd expect. But as a turd, I still have a lot of shit in my system I'd like to clean out. Take out on you, more specifically. Are you game?"

"Betcha. Anytime."

"Now." Thad motioned toward the west end of the ranch layout. "That stand of cottonwoods yonder should be nice and private. Let's take a stroll over there. . . ."

The two of them headed that way at an idle pace, neither man wanting to attract the attention of anyone who might chance to be watching them.

They passed an open-sided hay shed where the Patchwork Man was squatting in its shade, using a sharp knife to flense the bear hide of Janeece's latest kill for curing. He briefly glanced up at them, then went back to his work.

Nobody, unless it was R. B. himself, knew his real name. Everyone called him the Patchwork Man, or Patchy for short, because of his blend of different races. God knew who or what he really was. Except that had been Janeece's servant and general factotum on all his hunting trips, as far back as Thad could remember.

Patchy was a squat and strongly-built man who was rumored to have a mixture of white and black and Mexican and Creek Indian blood in his veins, along with a dash of Chinese. He was a downright ugly fellow whose face was gnarled by old scars, and more scars showed on the forearms revealed by his uprolled sleeves. No way of telling what his real age might be. The Patchwork Man hardly ever spoke, and then only in slurred gutturals, accompanied by various gestures

70

that only R. B. Janeece seemed to understand. Patchy's usual garb was a grimy, white cotton shirt and trousers and tall Apache moccasins; his mane of long, black hair was confined at his brow by a red headband deeply ingrained with filth.

"Somethin', ain't he," Hurd remarked colorlessly.

Thad said, "That he is," just as indifferently.

The grove of cottonwood trees grew in a long flanking arm along one end of the ranch yard. The growth was so dense and underbrushed that the two men could get behind it only by skirting widely. Then it cut them off completely from view of any building on the headquarters proper.

Thad pulled to a stop and said, "Here'll be fine," as he shed his buckskin coat and draped it carefully over a projecting limb. "All right with you?"

Hurd merely raised his brows in a sleepy-eyed assent and stood flat-footed, just waiting. His thick arms hung loosely alongside his barrel-built trunk. His expression was so patiently stolid that he looked almost bored.

Thad was wary of Hurd's impenetrable indifference; somehow it seemed superior even to a contempt of his opponent. He might have a few surprises up his sleeve. God knew he wasn't stupid, and he might be able to move faster than his squatly clumsy bulk would suggest.

Thad moved in carefully, his fists cocked, shuffling a little from side to side. Sporting around with buddies, he had engaged in a few friendly

71

sparring matches. He'd even picked up some professional tips from a hard-drinking Australian ex-boxer in Cheyenne, and he'd learned he could move quickly and hit hard.

But Hurd . . . Hurd was an unknown quantity. Something about his implacable stolidity was unnerving. It might be a calculated facade intended to disconcert an adversary. Thad didn't doubt that Hurd would be utterly merciless with any foe he ever got at a disadvantage.

So would I, Thad thought. So would Uncle Bob. That knowledge touched him with a steadying, if guarded, confidence.

He flicked a straight-armed jab at Hurd's jaw, a jaw sunk into the neckless granite of his trunk. For Thad it was just a testing shot.

Hurd jerked his head sideways, not enough to elude the blow but enough to slip nearly all its force past his head. Damn. The bugger was fast enough, all right. *So hit him even faster!*

Without an instant's hesitation, Thad bored in and drove his left fist into Hurd's gut in a mild feint, then slammed his other fist straight into Hurd's nose. He immediately sprang back out of Tancred's reach.

God! The man just stood there as immobile as a rock, his hands not even stirring from his sides. He coughed gently and ignored the rivulet of blood trickling from one side of his squashed-looking nose. He had been hit there before.

Thad felt a touch of murderous fury as he smashed three thudding blows to Hurd's middle, standing close to him, keeping his own head ducked. He slammed a right and a left and another right to Hurd's face, a barrage that should have sent an ordinary man to the ground.

With Tancred, it didn't cause him even to retreat a step. It was like battering a mass of solid lard and bone.

A man couldn't uppercut Hurd's chinless head, so Thad hooked another vicious blow into his nose. It split open the other side and caused a second trickle of blood to flow into the first one. They ran together along Hurd's thick lips.

He raised an arm and sleeved the blood away. It was the first movement he'd made with either arm.

God Almighty, thought Thad, who had already stepped quickly back. Was the man even *human?*

Hurd didn't show a trace of distress. He simply dropped the arm back to his side and stood waiting. Again.

Thad knew that his own dismay, and some of the sudden panic he felt, must be showing on his face. Abruptly he felt as helpless as a child.

"Well, sonny," Tancred said tonelessly. It wasn't even a question.

"Hurd, you're quite an animal."

"I take that as a compliment." Hurd's mouth tipped up at the corners in the grotesque hint of a smile. He spit a little blood. "Let's just say it ain't 'pigface' no more. Or 'piggy.' "

"All right."

"I'm the boss?"

"You're the boss." Thad's pride compelled him to add, "For as long as you can make it stick. But, hell, you know that."

"We both do. Here on, I'll have eyes in the back o' my head where you're concerned, sonny. We know that, too."

"Sure." Thad lifted his jacket off the limb and shrugged into it, watching Hurd. "All right if I'm 'Thad' from now on? No 'sonny.'"

"Reckon you got your share of good sense along with all that sand in your craw. Long as you don't get reckoning you can walk on water."

"Not till I get my growth."

"Okay with me, sonny. I mean Thad."

For the first, and probably the only, time, the two gave each other faintly genuine grins. Though Thad knew it was an acknowledgment of defeat on his part.

That was all right; it evened off to a truce of sorts. They understood each other fine. But Thad's hatred for the RBJ foreman had now thickened till it had a brassy taste on his tongue.

And both men were aware of that, too.

CHAPTER SEVEN

Gage Cameron was still full of raw twinges when he rolled out of his bunk late morning. He had slept like a log, unstirring, and the propped-open book on his chest fell to the floor. He stared at it owlishly, feeling the scatter of nuggets that had rolled onto the shuck mattress, gouging his hips.

"Gage? You up?" Amber called from the common room.

He rasped a reply; his mouth tasted like a burned-out kiln.

Grimacing against his aches and pains, Gage gathered up the ore samples and jammed them into his pocket.

After a moment's hesitation he went to the small bureau at the foot of his bed, opened a drawer, and dug among its assorted contents till he found his *bizha,* the personal amulet or fetish that old Adakhai had given him when he was a boy, assuring him that it was powerful medicine. He hadn't worn it in a dozen years. It was made of turquoise because Noholike, the god of gambling, had been successful with it. And you are a gambler, Adakhai told him. That you will always be.

True enough. He liked long chances taken

against long shots. Cautious, always weighing the chances against the odds. But enjoying the game all the same.

Gage hung the fetish from his belt by its rawhide thong. He also got out a clean shirt and pulled it on.

Then he parted the drape, walked out to the common room, and returned Bernewitz's book to its shelf. He went to the counter and plunged a dipper into the water bucket. He thirstily gulped down three dippers of water, one after the other.

"Something to eat?" Amber, who looked quite fetching in a worn but fresh calico dress, was bustling back and forth about her usual tasks.

"Uh-huh," Gage said.

She hung the coffeepot on the trammel hook above the fireplace coals, then set out a plate of cold bacon and eggs and corn bread. Either you got to breakfast on time, or it was served cold except for the coffee, Gage thought. He discovered that he was ravenously hungry; after his breakfast he drank two scalding cups of coffee and felt halfway human again.

"Where's Ran?"

"God knows," Amber said. "Out huntin' again, I suppose. The old man's still abed. Naturally. What's your day gonna be about, Gage?"

Gage drained his cup. "I plan to pay a call on old Adakhai."

She turned an incredulous stare on him, eyed the *bizha* dangling from his belt, then flashed a gleaming smile. "You must aim to make tall medicine with the old poop."

"Maybe." Gage smiled back at her. "Gal, how would you like a brand-new dress? Maybe a couple of 'em?"

"*New?* Gee, that *would* be a change. Are you serious?"

"Try me later," Gage said. He rose, picked up his rifle, and lounged out to the porch, limping only a little as he headed for the outback.

While he relieved himself on the one holer, he took out his knife and the nuggets. He carefully applied the tests for pyrite, pyrrhotite, and chalcopyrite. Once more he felt a glow of excitement. This was true gold; it stood up splendidly to each test.

Afterward Gage went to the corral, saddled his roan, and started north through the upsloping timber toward the upper plateau.

Scattered widely across it was the loose aggregate of hogans occupied by the Navaho and their half-breed relatives. "Dogtown," the white people in the low country called it, and the name fit. It was a lonesome and impoverished settlement, isolated far to the north of Canyon de Chelly, where Colonel Kit Carson and his troops had brought the Navaho to defeat in their own hereditary stronghold.

Mungo Cameron, as a young man, had come to Wyoming with his bride, Morning Light, and their infant son, Gage, to visit his friend Hermann Gottlieb, whose life he had once saved when they had both shipped before the mast on the high seas in the 1850s. By now Gottlieb, rough, ruthless, and enterprising, had owned a huge spread, which he had developed by having the men of his crew file land under the Homestead Act, the Preemption Act, and the Timber Culture Act, then waiting out whatever time the law specified before they could sell, and he could buy them out, for a few dollars.

But true to his own lights, Gottlieb had felt he owed an overwhelming debt to his old friend Cameron and so had deeded over to him the lush uplands north of his outfit. It had been a perfectly legal contract; by now both Mungo Cameron and Hermann Gottlieb were naturalized American citizens. Mungo had returned to the Corn River reservation and had escorted most of his wife's clan relatives north to Wyoming, where they might settle and raise sheep.

Altogether it hadn't worked out badly. By then the Navaho were a sullen lot of dispirited and played-out reservation refugees. Isolated from the main body of their tribe, they had let the worst of the white man's practices infiltrate their lives. They'd taken to heavy drinking, had lost a grip on their traditional culture, and had fallen into slovenly and indifferent ways.

Yet there had never been any real antagonism between the Cameron and Gottlieb land holdings, even after R. B. Janeece had bought up Gottlieb's ranch. The men would amicably work together to separate their own strayed herds or flocks, come roundup times.

Gage bleakly wondered if, in the light of recent developments, all that would change.

He came to a scattered flock of sheep that was largely watched over by the three men of the Cameron crew, the Hurteen brothers, Joe, Sull, and Billy. All were full-blood Navaho who enjoyed their lazy, idyllic work and were thoroughly acquainted with the white man's vices, even to adjusting to the convenience of taking American first names.

Gage rode around the flock, saying an *ahalani*, or hello, to each man he met. He always enjoyed the three brothers, amiable look-alikes who might almost have been triplets. Like him, they were in their late twenties. They cruised through life like feathers in the wind but otherwise were dependable men, who were loyal to the Camerons and performed their duties without reproach. Why not? They received a comfortable salary for their simple needs and otherwise didn't give much of a damn for anything.

"*Ahalani, anaai!*" Sull whooped in greeting. "Hey, Gage! How you doin' nowadays? Gettin' any?"

"Any what?"

Sull laughed. "You go out and hunt, roam the country, do what you want, you an' Ran, huh? We do all the work for you guys."

"Sure. You boys seems to like it so damn much. Not wanting for anything, are you?"

Another easygoing rumble of a laugh from Sull.

Gage rode on, grinning. Privately he felt a touch of shame.

That was indeed how he and Ran conducted their lives, doing what they pleased when they pleased. What damned business did he have passing judgment on anyone? Gage was divided between ambitions for his own family and a personal admission that he himself was committed to a slack and unchanging way of existence. Often, when he got thinking about it, he was troubled. But he liked his personal freedom — what would he be without it?

Gage crossed a couple of heavily brushed ridges and saw below him a spare layout of hogans. This was the camp of Adakhai and his near kin. Spirals of smoke curled up from the fires and bore with them the odors of wood smoke, of the strong smells of sumac and pinon gum, of the greasy taint of mutton being broiled. All of it was familiar to him, and he rode down into the camp.

Two of Adakhai's young granddaughters greeted him with pleasure as he rode up to Adakhai's hogan. Actually, according to Navaho custom, it was the hereditary lodge of his last wife. But there was never any doubt that Adakhai presided over it and this whole small conclave of Navaho. The stacked-up house was a large hogan made of pine logs, boughs, and cedar and showed a degree of the white man's influence. It boasted somewhat more in room and comfort than the old-style, forked-together hogans whose structure the Talking God had decreed ages before.

Gage dismounted before Adakhai's lodge and threw his horse's reins. One of the granddaughters went into the lodge ahead of him to notify Adakhai of his visit. Shortly she peered out and, at her beckoning sign of assent, Gage ducked through the low doorway and entered.

A trench full of banked coals glowed in the middle of the dirt floor. Adakhai sat cross-legged on a sheepskin pallet at its far side. The granddaughter retreated from the hogan.

"*Xoxo nanaxi, Hatali,*" Gage said in respectful greeting. "Long life and happiness, man of medicine."

"*Ahalani, tineh,*" Adakhai said with equal formality, his voice rustling like dry leaves. "Greetings, young man."

Gage had an eerie feeling that it was almost as though the ancient shaman had been expecting him. *Maybe he had.*

Gage seated himself cross-legged on the near side of the fire trench. "I have come to ask your counsel, *Hatali.*"

The old man dipped his head in a bare assent. There would be none of the usual Navaho ceremony about this visit. One way in which both men were alike was their scorn for ceremonial greetings.

Adakhai's shrunken and withered frame was wrapped in a *yei,* a medicine man's blanket. His white hair hung over his shoulders, framing a

81

face that was wrinkled as a prune and nearly as dark. His small black eyes rested on Gage's *bizha*.

"You wear your medicine after so long," he said huskily.

"Yes."

Gage told him of what had happened yesterday in the deserted camp by the Los Pinos, and he was careful to omit no detail. If Adakhai was to be of any help, there could be no deceiving him. He, and only he, must know about the gold. Also, Gage was assailed by a usual uncanny sense that his mind and heart lay open to the ancient shaman.

When he'd heard him out, Adakhai picked up a stick at his side and prodded at the coals in the fire.

"It is not well," he said at last. "That place is *cikoha*. It is sacred ground. This you knew."

"Yes."

"You have never believed, *tineh*. Do you believe now?"

Gage hesitated. "I do not know what to believe. I tell you only what I saw and felt. My heart is open."

"It may be the beginning of wisdom." Adakhai poked at the coals some more. Smoke began to wisp up from the end of the stick. "None of the white-eyes' ways you have learned in the East tell you?"

"None." Gage spread his hands, which were resting on his knees, slightly open. "They have their god. Our people have gods. None have spoken to me. How do I know?"

"Your head is closed."

"My heart is open."

"Your head is closed," Adakhai repeated. "The *Belinkana* did this for you."

"They know many things that the *Dineh* never learned." Gage said stubbornly. "You cannot say these are false things. I have seen them, *Hatali*."

"Great villages of stone? I have heard of these."

"Yes."

"*Pesh-e-gar,* the guns? Big ships on the big water? The iron horse that travels on iron trails? The whispering wires that carry messages from far places?"

"Yes. And many more things."

Adakhai continued to prod at the ruddy glow of the cherried coals. The banked fires burst suddenly into a single sheet of clean flame that erupted upward for two feet. Gage flinched backward instinctively, hands closing tight on his knees.

"*Look, tineh!*"

Now a thin vomit of smoke was swirling up to screen the flame. Gage stared. He blinked. He saw images swimming among the flames and smoke . . . and he knew them.

There were the two-story barracks and officers' quarters of the old army post in Pennsylvania that had become the Carlisle Indian Industrial School. Even to an illusory and fleeting picture of the old army bandstand that stood to one side of the parade ground. He saw other things, too, in quick succession. Clipper ships with their towering masts and numerous squares of unfurled canvas. He saw a locomotive charging straight at him, funneling a plume of smoke.

All of it was largely obscured in the confusion of flame and smoke, but he couldn't doubt that images of his own memory had been conjured up to his vision.

Gage let out a grunted expletive — *"Juth la hage ni!"* — and threw one forearm up to cover his eyes. The oath was a particularly vile one on the Navaho tongue. Almost at once he wondered if he would be forgiven for saying it.

Cautiously he lowered his arm. The smoke was gone. The sheet of flame had ebbed back to a layer of twinkling coals.

"Do you know what you have seen?" Adakhai asked tonelessly.

Gage felt a sudden and unreasoning rage toward this ancient one who croaked like a bird of ill omen. Somehow Adakhai had been able to do the thing deliberately. "I saw," he said huskily, hating an awareness that his voice was shaking a little. "*Hatali* might have done this before. There were times."

"There were times. But you were a child. Children always believe. Later they think they learn and they are no longer children. All men speak for the Great Power in their way. The *Belinkana* have one way. It is not the way of the *Dineh*."

"I am half white-eyes."

"Still, you are one of the *Dineh*. With you it cannot be otherwise. It is of the blood. Maybe it would be different with another. But you are *Dineh*."

"What do these words mean?"

"What you saw may be the shadows of your own head. Maybe they have been there a long time. You are angry, *tineh*."

Damn the enigmatic old bastard. He might be able to command supernatural powers, or maybe he only had a mesmeric ability to draw out another's thoughts. Either way, he would reveal no more of his precious medicine secrets than he had to.

"Yes. But if Adakhai knows that, he knows I came to seek truth. Not mockeries half hidden in smoke."

For the first time Gage thought he saw a glimmer of amusement in the old man's deep-socketed eyes.

"It is well said. Then hear me, *tineh*. The whites do not hold to the ways of their fathers. They always want to change that which has always been. They are a hungry people. They would eat the earth." Adakhai paused, hacking an old man's wheeze of a cough. "Their ways are putrid. Even their Power must hate the stink of them. What is this *pesh-litzog*, this yellow iron? What do they call it?"

"Gold."

"Gold. It is the earth. They would sell even the earth, the mother of all things. They have corrupted the bodies of our people with their ways. But the spirits cannot be corrupted. They have told you this. You are half *Dineh* and half white-eyes. You are like a bat, *tineh;* you are neither bird nor mouse. So they may speak to your Navaho part, even as they warn your *Belinkana* half. That they cannot change."

Gage hesitated again. "Then . . . what must I do?"

"If you want the *pesh-litzog* so much?"

"Yes."

"Yours is a kind spirit. You do not want this *gold* for yourself. They know. Therefore, you must go to the *cikoha* where you buried it and take it up. Take it to another place. Do not disturb the sacred ground again."

"That is all?" Gage asked.

"It is enough. I do not know what might be done to you — *or others* — if they touch the sacred ground again." Adakhai raised his corded and withered arm and stabbed out a bony forefinger. *"But be warned."*

There was still enough time before sunset for Gage to make a hurried trip back to the deserted camp above the west bank of the Los Pinos River where he had buried the gold cache.

Nothing in the world could have tempted him to visit the place after dark.

He dismounted from his roan close to the spot and tied him to a stem of brush in plain sight. For a moment he stood fingering his turquoise

86

bizha. Then he took his saddlebags and tramped on to where he had left the gold buried, next to the nearly submerged grinning skull.

Not even glancing at the skull, or not daring to, Gage dug down to the nuggets and gold flakes. He didn't take time to rub them free of dirt as he transferred them to his saddlebags.

As he straightened up from his task, he felt it again. A murmurous rush of air that stirred the brush . . . and yet it was not a real wind.

Gage stood with his feet apart, waiting. But this time there was nothing of cold menace or foreboding in the rush of air. It blew warmly across his face. It might have been an unbidden note of approval.

He glanced at his horse. The gelding was nuzzling calmly at the brush, undisturbed.

Gage walked back and slung the saddlebags over his pommel. Then he mounted up and swung the roan gelding around. All he wanted was to get away from here, fast.

CHAPTER EIGHT

Gage rode into the small town of Glade late next morning.

It was a typical white man's village, no bigger than one would expect to find anywhere on this back end of nowhere, up close to the Neversummer peaks. There was a general merchandise store, a feed company, a blacksmith shop, a livery stable, a few undesignated buildings, and a cramped little shack that served as the U. S. Land Office. All of them occupied one side of a muddy, wagon-mired trace that was the settlement's only street.

Gage dismounted in front of the land office building, tied his horse at the rail, and tramped onto the porch. He rapped twice at the door. Scott Everston's tired and irritable voice said, "Come in."

Gage entered.

The room was a mess. Books and papers were strewn all over. Scott Everston was on his hands and knees, gathering them up in an obvious effort to find the right places to file them back where they belonged.

Scott glanced up. "Hello, Gage."

"What's happened here?"

"The place was broken into last night, and our papers got rifled through." Scott motioned bitterly at the room's one single-paned window; the glass had been broken and the shards had fallen inward. "He came in that way, whoever it was. He must have been looking for something. What the hell was it?"

Gage had to think it over for only about fifteen seconds. Then he said quietly, "I can make a guess."

"Make it then, dammit!"

Gage nodded at the table in one corner. "That where you keep all your charts of folks who've registered land claims?"

Scott Everston rose slowly to his feet, frowning a little. "Yes, sure. Just about everyone here-abouts knows that. But what —"

"See if you can find any that apply to the open range west of the RBJ spread."

Scott went to the table and sorted quickly through the charts. Then he said suddenly, "The devil! One's missing. Gone. Just that one chart —"

"Did it show where Reeve Bedoe's claim is?"

"Yes, but . . . oh." Scott's puzzled frown ironed out. "He's the black man."

"Yeah. Want to sit down, Scott? I'll tell you."

Gage settled into a chair facing the small office desk with its disordered clutter of papers. After a moment Scott slumped into the chair behind it. "Well?" he said dejectedly.

Scott Everston was a thin young man, slight

89

of build, with an unruly thatch of rust-colored hair. He wore a shabby gray corduroy suit and had the pallor of a man who spent most of his time indoors, though his freckled face was mildly sunburned. A pair of thick-lensed spectacles rested on his bony nose, and he blinked through them almost continually. Scott was an assistant government surveyor for this part of the territory. He was also one of the few close friends Gage had among the white men he knew.

"Can't say for sure," Gage told him. "But I think it's a pretty sure guess. . . ."

He told Scott everything that had happened to him over the past twenty-four hours, again omitting any mention of his gold find — and his visit to Adakhai. He also told Scott what he suspected about the theft of the land chart.

Scott scrubbed a hand over his jaw, nodding slowly. "Well . . . that would explain it, all right. RBJ wants to roust Reeve Bedoe off his homestead. So they, one of their men anyway, busted in here and swiped the chart. But why the hell did they have to wreck my office?"

"Maybe," Gage said, "because they wanted to find out if you had any other documents on hand that would testify to Bedoe's occupancy of that claim."

Scott shook his head. "There aren't any. Those charts contain the whole record of my land registrations. Damn!" He took off his glasses and rubbed a hand across his brow. "I should have sent copies of all those charts to the U. S. Land

Office in Washington. To date I haven't done so. I've been remiss. But, my God, I never expected anything of this sort!"

"Forget it," Gage said. "What's done is done. What we have to think about now is heading the bastards off. If you're game."

"Anything." Scott dropped the hand from his forehead and eyed Gage quizzically. "But what brought you into town today? Something you wanted to see me about?"

Gage nodded. "It can wait. Right now I think both of us had better pay a call on Reeve Bedoe. And I mean *now*. Oh . . . and bring along your transit."

At midafternoon the two men came upon the Bedoe homestead claim. In a few minutes they rode into the place. Reeve Bedoe wasn't about to be caught off guard by anyone this time. He'd been out working on his outsheds but left off work and was standing ready, rifle in his hands, as they rode up.

Recognizing both Gage and Scott, he let his rifle slack down; a broad smile of greeting broke on his dark face. He invited the two of them to step down and come into the house.

The log-walled interior was a single large room, crudely furnished but kept impeccably clean. Opal was fixing supper, and she welcomed both men warmly. Ordinarily she might be an aloof and perhaps a somewhat shy woman, but once she'd accepted someone, her reserved dignity thawed.

Reeve broke out a half-full bottle of good Kentucky sour mash and three cups and held the bottle poised over them, grinning almost mischievously. "Neither you boys got any objection to a little kick o' the mule, have you?" He winked at Gage. "*You* ain't, have you?"

Gage smiled. "I guess I can stand one this time around. You, Scott?"

"I'm not known for resisting any such offer," Scott Everston said. "But is this a private joke between you?"

"You might say that." Reeve grinned. He carried the cups to the table and half filled each one. The three men sat down, mildly saluted one another with the cups, and drank.

"I think you men would do well to stay with one drink apiece," Opal said a little tartly as she went back and forth between the stove and the makeshift crib where her baby lay, kicking his feet and cooing lustily.

"What's his name, ma'am?" Scott asked.

"Ishmael," Opal said. "Right out of the Old Testament. Here" — she stuck a "sugartit," a hunk of sugar wrapped in a linsey cloth, in the baby's mouth — "nurse on that and be still."

Gage nodded gravely, remembering that Ishmael and his mother had been the outcast son and wife of Abraham. "It fits, I reckon."

"It fits for sure," Reeve said, ignoring his wife's advice and splashing more liquor into each cup. "You boys drink up now. And tell me what brung you both here same time. Wouldn't reckon it's just a social call . . . is it?"

Reeve already knew what Gage had told him a couple of days ago. His brows drew tightly; he was faintly scowling as Scott related how the land office had been broken into and a particular chart had been stolen.

"What you figure," he said finally, slowly, "is them RBJ folks aim to bind my black ass in a real vise."

"Reeve!" Opal said sharply.

Reeve shook his head, still scowling. "Sorry, honeybunch. Give an oath I try to watch my language, specially now we got a kid. But god-*damn*, men! Sounds like that RBJ bunch is all set to nail my black hide first of all. If they can wipe me out . . ."

"That's part of it," Scott agreed. "But Gage and I see it as the first step in what will be a concerted effort on their part to clear out *all* homesteaders this side of the Los Pinos River. It's all public-domain grass, open to any 'steaders that can stake a legal U. S. government claim here. They merely aim to make you a prime example because you're nearest them. And, of course, because you and yours are Negroes."

Reeve twirled his glass between thick fingers. "Yeah . . . I see that right enough. What do I do?"

"That's why we came here right away, Reeve," Gage said. "If they make a move, it should come soon. Quite probably today. We'll be here to side you."

"You reckon that'll be enough?"

Gage smiled faintly. "It had better be. We don't have any additional troops to call on."

Reeve laughed shortly. "Yeah. Well, I'm obliged to you gentlemen. Meantime we just wait?"

Gage nodded. "Just that."

Scott cleared his throat. "One thing I'm curious about, Mr. Bedoe. I can see you've gone to great lengths to make the required improvements on your claim. But nothing to indicate what you intend to do with it. I presume you plan to farm —"

"I do. First off, I figure to raise a few woollies. Not many. Just aim to have a small flock of 'em brought in shortly."

Gage and Scott exchanged brief glances, and then Scott said quietly, "That's up to you. But it'll make matters worse. Sheep and cattle don't mix, according to most cattlemen."

"Yeah." Reeve poured himself another half cup of liquor and swigged it down. "That's what they always say. But it ain't true. Sure, sheep crop the grass off short, but the shorter it gets, the better it grows up fresh and green next spring, all the better for cattle. Hell, I herded sheep long enough in the Nations to know that."

"Fine," Scott said dryly. "If you can convince the cowman."

"Well, Mr. Everston, maybe they come swarming all over me if I don't do what *they* want. But I'm gonna do what *I* want."

94

Reeve's face held a stubborn set. Gage could respect his tough tenacity, but it was the kind that cost a man dearly. Argue with him and it would only worsen matters.

They all straightened up at the sound of approaching horses. Reeve picked up his rifle and walked to the open door and stepped outside. Gage and Scott followed him out and stood flanking him on either side.

Four men. Two of them were Thad Overmile and Hurd Tancred, the RBJ ramrod. Another was a stony-faced fellow whom Gage remembered as one of the three he'd surprised on his earlier visit here. He didn't know the fourth rider, a chunky and red-faced man who wore a deputy sheriff's badge on his faded vest.

"Light down," Reeve said. "This a sociable call, Mr. Overmile? Or you fellas come to pick up your property? I got two ropes, a whip, and a hat you left behind last visit."

Thad made no move to dismount; his glance flicked over the three of them. Plainly he hadn't expected anything like this. "No, this is business. But the message is the same. You're squatting here, Uncle. We want you off. This time I've brought the law to back me. And we're his deputies. We've all been officially sworn."

"That red-faced man the law? You got him." Reeve nodded to his left and his right. "Me, I got friends."

"So I see," Thad said thinly. "Even to the land office clerk. What are you doing here, Everston?"

"One of our survey charts is missing," Scott said. "Our office was ransacked last night and one chart stolen. It showed the registration of Mr. Bedoe's homestead. He's no squatter, Overmile."

Thad's face held a barely contained fury. "Can you prove it?"

"Yes," Scott said calmly. "I registered his claim myself. I'm a witness to the fact. I'll testify as much if I'm brought to court. Who would any *honest* judge believe, you or me? By the way, Overmile, you and the *other* deputies have no authority on federal land, even if it's within the county. You'd have to bring in the U. S. Marshal for this territory to arbitrate the matter."

Thad flushed; he reined in his restless mount. That was another thing he hadn't taken into consideration. Hard to tell what Hurd Tancred was thinking; his flat, thick face showed nothing.

Thad said softly, "You're not accusing us of stealing that chart?"

"In front of witnesses? Of course not," Scott said blandly. "How do I know who stole it? All that Mr. Cameron and I are doing here is paying a call on a friend."

"Like hell!"

"Prove it."

Thad flicked a wicked glance at Gage. "You wouldn't be one of the jaspers who opened up on us from that ridge yonder a couple days ago, would you?"

Gage smiled. "I was *one*, yes."

"You show real good sense in choosing allies, Everston," Thad said with a savage irony. "A nigger and a half-breed Injun. It won't win you a lot of friends in these parts!"

"No," Scott agreed mildly. "Not among your like. Small loss."

The stony-faced man moved his mount over by the visitors' horses, gazing curiously at the elaborate canvas case containing Scott's transit and its tripod. These were lashed onto a spare horse. He reached out a hand.

"What's this here, now?"

"It's a transit," Scott said tautly. "Don't touch it. It's a costly instrument and not easily replaceable."

"Oh . . . yeah. That's what you land office guys survey with."

"Breck!" Hurd Tancred spoke for the first time, shifting his massive barrel of a body in his saddle. His voice was flat and expressionless. "Leave it alone."

Breck drew his revolver in a lightning-fast motion; he tapped the transit with its barrel. Gage's Winchester was cocked. He whipped it up and fired, quick as thought.

The slug seared the rump of Breck's horse; it squealed and careened crazily around. First the animal crashed sidelong into Thad's mount and then, veering farther sideways, into Tancred's. All three men had to fight wildly to bring their horses under control.

When they had finally settled down, Breck

twisted in his saddle to face Gage.

Breck's revolver was cocked but not yet leveled. He was already looking straight down the barrel of Gage's rifle, levered and ready, aimed at his head.

"Go on," Gage told him. "Go ahead."

"Dammit — let it go, Breck!" Thad said wrathfully. "All right, Uncle. You've won your point. *This time.*"

Breck was staring cold-eyed at Gage. Slowly he let his revolver off-cock and sheathed it, and he came close to smiling. "Maybe we two will meet again."

"That'll be your choice," Gage said.

"You're trespassin'," Reeve put in. "Better get off. A man can shoot a trespasser. Law says so."

"Just so," Thad murmured. "But you have to live on it for a half year before it's yours, coon cat."

Reeve raised a hand politely. "One moment, sir, if you please."

He tramped into the house and returned with two ropes, a whip, and a hat, which he handed up to Thad, who snatched them almost viciously from his hands.

They watched the four men turn their horses and ride away.

"Whee-oo!" Reeve grinned at Gage and Scott. "That was a mighty close one."

"It could hit a lot closer," Scott said soberly. "Mr. Bedoe, I'd advise against your bringing in any more sheep, even a few. You have a wife

98

and baby to think about. Not just yourself."

"Yeah," Reeve said slowly. "I thought about that. But *damn,* men. I can't abide any son of a bitch telling me what I can or can't do."

Several hours of daylight remained, and Gage and Scott spent them verifying where the east boundary of the RBJ property ran along a stretch of open grass. Gage served as Scott's chain man. Finally Scott folded his tripod and packed it away on his spare horse, carefully wedging his transit alongside it.

"There's no doubt of it," he said. "RBJ's property does overlap the Los Pinos River on this side. It reaches about one hundred yards west of it, confirming the original U. S. survey. That what you wanted to know?"

Gage nodded. The old *cikoha* of the Navaho lay well within the RBJ line. He would have to lay his plans for getting the gold out damned carefully. "That's it," he said.

Scott showed a wry and sardonic smile. "But I still don't understand why you were so curious about *this* boundary line. It's way southwest of your Cameron holdings. Can't affect you in any way."

"Not directly," Gage said. "But it matters. You'll have to take my word on it, Scott. For now."

"All right." Scott kicked glumly at the rich-grassed turf. "I like Reeve Bedoe. There's a man. But I'm afraid he's setting his family and himself up for a whole mess of trouble with RBJ. God knows how it will come, but it will."

"I can't argue that. But he's bound to take his chances. I guess so is his wife."

"Dammit, why? He's not a stupid man!"

"Far from it. But he was born into slavery, Scott. That can warp a man's thinking all his life. Now he's gotten to where he'd rather take a long chance than compromise by even an inch." Gage stared across the rolling plain to the west, the blades of grass rippled by a late afternoon breeze. "And I can't say as I blame him."

CHAPTER NINE

The next morning Gage undertook the task of inspecting the steep surface of incline on the lower part of the Los Pinos River for more signs of gold.

Keeping a wary surveillance on all sides of him, he went about his preparations with stealthy and elaborate care. First, after taking breakfast, he hunted through an old tack shed crammed full of some of the family's pack-rat possessions.

A rewarding search. Gage scoured up three serviceable lariats and a couple of old lanterns, along with a rusty hatchet and a large can of coal oil. While daylight still held, he surreptitiously conveyed these to the critical spot on the rimrock overlooking the Los Pinos.

Gage fastened the two lanterns on one of the fifty-foot ropes, positioning them about twenty feet apart. He made an elaborate network of rope from another of the lariats and suspended the lanterns in such a way that there'd be no danger of either one getting scorched or burning through the main rope.

In the third line of rope he tied thick knots at roughly one-foot intervals. He had already sized up a pair of massive rocks along the rimrock to which the lariats could be safely fastened. After securing the rope ends to the huge boulders, set about four feet apart, Gage went home for supper.

As usual, the family showed little curiosity about his comings and goings. Amber displayed a mild inquisitiveness but didn't really care. Ran was totally indifferent. Old Mungo simply retreated into his usual booze-fed drowsiness.

So far so good.

Gage returned to the site by the Los Pinos as sunset was washing the sky. He reached it by late twilight. Working by the last fading light, he charged the two lanterns with coal oil and lit them. Then, taking great care, he lowered the rock-anchored line down along the cliffside to its full length.

Now he lowered the second rope, the one with knots in it, down alongside the first one. He was satisfied with the somewhat fitful illumination that the suspended lanterns would provide him.

With the hatchet shoved in his belt, Gage slipped over the rim and let himself down easily, hand over hand, clinging to the knotted rope. He didn't go far at first. He started out just below the rimrock, hacking carefully with the hatchet at the incline to either side of him, knocking free clods of dirt and rock that rattled down the escarpment into the darkness below.

It was easy going, on the whole.

The ground was loose, for whole sections had been bared by recent collapsings of the outer surface. These had liberated the chunks of gold-bearing quartz that Gage had found earlier.

And, he now discovered exultantly, there was plenty more where these had come from. He saw the racing sparkle of lantern light on many clods as they crumbled under repeated strokes of his hatchet.

Gage lowered himself gradually along the line as he worked, always gripping a knot in the rope with one hand, while with the other he whacked hard and steadily at the steep slope on each side.

He was getting good results, and this lent a labored excitement to his efforts, his breath whistling out between his teeth. So did the nervous knowledge that each blow of the hatchet might detach another section of cliff wall from above and bring the whole mass cascading down on him.

His arms grew tired. One from hanging on to the rope, the other from laboriously and awkwardly slamming the hatchet blade into the cliffside.

Despite his youth and strength, Gage felt the great strain on his muscles. At various times he had to haul himself back to the rim and rest a while. Once rested, he could resume the work. The knots he'd made in the rope enabled him to ascend it quickly, then descend again to continue his dogged labors.

When the first hint of dawn began to gray in the east, he wearily left off work. He hauled both lines up the rim and laid them out flat so that no ordinary observer who chanced on the spot by daylight and viewed it from across the river would catch any sign of what he was doing.

Afterward Gage trudged upriver to the point where he could climb down to the ledge of collapsed rubble. Then he worked back downriver to where he could inspect, by the early morning light, all the pieces of rock he had knocked down.

Again he felt the surge of excitement. He was filthy rich now.

Once more Gage packed up the best pieces of gold-studded quartz, this time in a flour sack he'd brought to the cache place upriver, well away from the riverbank and the eerily haunted Navaho camp. There he buried it. By then he was so dead tired that all he could do was throw himself down on the ground and go to sleep.

When he awoke, the sun was high in the sky and blazing hot. He was still aching in every muscle. It was all he could manage to do to limp back to where he had left his horse, packing the ropes and lanterns. Then he rode home, still utterly exhausted but deeply satisfied.

There might be a lot of gold quartz left embedded in the cliff below the point where he'd searched, at the limits of his rope lines. But why get too greedy? In a single night's work he had gathered enough of the precious stuff to make him and his wealthy for the rest of their lives.

All that remained was to sort it out and take the best to where he could secretly have it converted into the best return in solid cash. And there was no hurry. He could have it done gradually. Over a period of months, even years.

Gage was content. He wouldn't have been if he had known what would follow.

CHAPTER TEN

For at least two days out of each week, Amber Cameron would quit her daily busywork around the outfit and take a day's vacation, riding wherever she wanted and doing what she pleased. Once in a while she might indulge in a mildly intense flirtation with one of the Navaho boys on the upper plateau . . . or with others if it suited her.

But like as not, she'd prefer to seek her personal favorite spot down the river, where she could spend much of a day diving and swimming in the water by herself. Here she could strip to the buff and purely enjoy herself as a free spirit.

Today Amber decided to swim. She pointed her bay toward the place on the Los Pinos River where she, Gage, and Ran would often go together on a hot summer day, back when they'd been some younger and had gotten along better.

The Swimhole, they had called the place. It was a wide backwater carved out of the riverbank below a shallow rise where dwarf pines had taken root in the crumbling talus, their branches crabbed and twisted, their lower trunks almost hidden by stiff clots of buck brush.

Amber rode through a break in the ridge and

came out above the river in a shallow clearing. She dismounted and tied Blackie's reins to a pine. Then she clambered down through a lacy barrier of fresh-leaved willows that draped a broad, flat, granite ledge in a kind of sylvan seclusion. The ledge, making a sharp drop-off above the Swimhole, could barely be seen.

In this backwater the current dissipated itself into a low swirl of water that was deep and dark, shot with beams of sunlight that never reached its bottom. Amber and her brothers had often tried to plumb its depth, but they could never dive as deep as its unknown floor. It was scary to think about how far down it might be, what might lurk there, but she loved this place. Coming here alone, she might drowse away an afternoon far from anything but the frolickings and chitterings of squirrels and jays.

Tired from swimming, she liked to sun herself on the ledge. Or laze away the pleasant hours with a cheap yellow-back novel, if she had one along. These slight books were full of romantic rubbish that bore no resemblance to life as she knew it, but reality hadn't crowded all the romantic notions out of her young head.

The water would be ice-cold. Fed by snowmelt out of the high Neversummers, it wouldn't be less cold on summer's hottest day. Amber shivered pleasurably as she shucked off her clothes, then shook down her cascade of glossy black hair.

She poised on the brink of the ledge, curling her toes against the sun-warmed rock, running her hands down her slim young flanks, bracing herself. She dived cleanly and deeply, letting her senses absorb the sudden shock of frigid water and darkness, then striking back to the surface.

Rolling on her back, she paddled languidly across the pool, enjoying the caress of water like icy silk along the brown-seal sleekness of her legs and loins, the streaming veil of her hair undulating over shoulders, over breasts like small bronze islands, over the dark nipples whose nubs had turned taut and impudent with water chill. She and her brothers had used to swim here a. (as Ran liked to put it), splashing about in water fights, having all kinds of fun, until Gage began to tease her in his sober-faced way, addressing her as "Miss Bumps," making her sadly and angrily aware that she couldn't be one of the boys any longer.

But Gage had honored her developing maturity, never venturing to the Swimhole if he knew she would be there. Afterward he'd soon left for his education stint at Carlisle in the East. But she'd sometimes suspected that Ran, or someone, was spying on her from the shallow ridge. Nothing she could put her finger on, just a feeling.

The little bastard — if it's him.

Amber dived again, deeply enough into tery black infinite below the light-shot water to slightly scare herself, before into a lithe upward arc and popped back face. She blew out air as she came up, and of her ascent making tickly bursts as she treaded water, slicking her hair back off her face with one hand.

That was when she heard the sound. Sharp and unmistakable. A crackle of brush, crisp and sudden, high on the wooded slope.

Then silence again.

Amber froze as she was except for the gentle tread water motions of her arms and legs. Her gaze quickly swept the slope, top to bottom and back again. It could have been an animal. But even as she thought about the possibility, she didn't believe it.

A heavy body had made that sound. It could have been a deer or an elk or a bear, or any sizable game beast. But a wild animal would not move in utter silence and so abruptly break it, then fall quiet again.

A man might. If he'd stolen up and had deliberately made a noise. A man who wanted to let her know he was spying on her.

Goose bumps quilled Amber's flesh. She treaded water a few moments longer, half paralyzed by more than the cold water. Then, fighting off panic, forcing herself not to hurry, she stroked around the pool in a leisurely circle, not even glancing toward the slope. Coming out of the water she'd be as naked as Eve to the watcher's eager gaze.

She thought, Dumbhead, he's already seen the altogether! He must have. Unless he'd come along just now. Hell, what's the difference?

109

You can't stay here forever!

Who was he? Ran? Some other Indian or half-breed. Maybe a white drifter?

One thing Amber knew. She wasn't going to dally by the pool and wait on what might happen. The sensible thing would be to clear out quickly and quietly, not seeming to be in a great hurry about it.

She stroked over by the ledge, then climbed up the slope alongside it. The crackle of brush came again, this time as a casual rustling. But its line of direction told her that whoever made it was coming straight her way.

She hastened to scramble into her clothes. . . .

CHAPTER ELEVEN

Thad Overmile was taking a solitary ride this morning. It was a pastime to which he was rarely given, as a rule. To himself, he could admit his real reason for doing so. He wanted to see if Amber Cameron was continuing her usual summer diversion of frequenting what she and her brothers called the Swimhole.

Today she might be there or she might not. Thad was hungering for a sight of her slim body glowing all naked and golden.

So far he hadn't managed it. This was because he had first encountered her on another ride of his, and they had idly bantered for a while, back and forth. Afterward he'd occasionally visited the Swimhole, hoping to catch her there alone. Once he'd actually done so, but she was fully dressed, just relaxing on the ledge, reading some trashy romance or other. Again they had exchanged banter, teasing each other, keeping the talk light and just short of friendly.

Very dissatisfying. Thad wanted more, and that Amber had continued to tease him unmercifully had only sharpened his appetite for her. He wanted that girl in the worst way.

This morning, coming up on the shallow ridge

overlooking the Swimhole, he heard a horse's faint whicker from the other side of it. Could be that was Amber's horse and she was there alone.

Thad chuckled silently. This time, instead of making a direct approach, he would steal up atop the ridge and, from its cover of brush and scrub trees, see what he could see. He dismounted, ground-hitched his horse, and climbed the low, easy slope, moving as quietly as he could. He came out at the crown of the ridge and, with a full view of the ledge above the Swimhole, sucked his breath into his lungs.

Amber was standing on the ledge, taking off her clothes. God, what a beauty she was! Her legs were still long and coltish but starting to round out beautifully. The sizable nuggets of her tan breasts showed promise of swelling into full globes. He watched avidly as she moved over to the lip of the ledge and made a quick, clean dive into the river pool.

Thad continued to watch for a while, entranced by the sight of her cavorting in the water, diving deep and then surfacing to paddle about, affording him many tantalizing glimpses of her body.

A wicked spark of mischief seized him.

Deliberately he broke a thick stem of brush, making a sharp noise that caused the girl to pause. She tried to cover her awareness by swimming slowly around the pool.

Thad was amused. He waited until Amber, obviously disconcerted, swam over to the slope be-

112

side the ridge. Now, briefly hidden from his view, she climbed up it. She stepped onto the ledge, and once again, his heart pounding wildly, Thad drank in the sight of her.

His wicked sense of fun caused him to reach out and break more brush, loudly.

He almost laughed out loud as Amber ran for her clothes. As she was getting into them, Thad climbed down off the ridge and confronted her on the ledge.

She was only partly clad, and she shot him an angry glare and continued to don her clothes, adding a blouse and pants and sandals to her drawers and chemise.

Then she straightened up to face him, saying clearly and bitterly, "Damn you! I might have known you'd do some more sneaking around here sometime."

"Seems you were right, missy," Thad drawled insolently. He sat down on his haunches about twenty feet from her, set his elbows on his knees, and laced his big hands loosely together, grinning his big, chalky grin.

"You set out to spy on me deliberate, didn't you!" Amber demanded.

"Well, of course. Why else you think I'd do it?" Thad settled down on his rump and began to pry off his boots.

"What are you *doing?*"

"Aiming to go for a swim my own self. Thought you might be hankering to join me."

"You go to hell!"

Thad grinned as he peeled off his socks. "Could be I'm already there, Miss Amber. You do know how to torment a man. You've done it to me before with your come-hither ways."

He was being a damned fool, Thad knew in the back of his mind. He was only antagonizing her now. But the urge was irresistible. Once he got onto these antic impulses, there was no controlling them.

"I suppose you seen quite a lot already," Amber said with an icy fury.

"Boy howdy. I should hope to offend the Almighty I have."

"I'll be leaving then," Amber said, swinging about and heading for her horse. "Have heaps of fun playing by yourself."

Thad was already unbuckling his belt to climb out of his trousers. "Hey!" he yelled, and sprinted across the ledge after her.

Amber shot a quick glance at him over her shoulder, then broke into a run. Thad made a dive at her, tackling her around the legs and bearing her down on the sun-warmed rock.

They rolled over and over, struggling wildly. All Thad could think of with her hot young contours writhing against him was to have Amber, to take her here and now. She was strong for a girl, but he was stronger. He was slowly subduing her, forcing her down on her back as he gripped her wrists, pinning them straight-armed above her head, confident of victory.

Then a shot came from the overlooking ridge.

It struck the rock ledge close to them and sang off in a screaming ricochet. Stinging chips peppered Thad's bare hide.

He swiveled a startled glance upward. He saw Ran Cameron standing amid the trees and brush above, his rifle trained. And he was levering to draw another bead.

God Almighty!

Unthinkingly Thad rolled away from Amber and sprang to his feet. Balling his body to a crouch, he raced for the brink of the ledge. Belatedly it flashed across his mind that he'd made a mistake; he should have kept hugging Amber close. Then Ran wouldn't dare shoot directly at him without risking his sister's life.

But the thought came too late.

Poised on the end of the ledge, Thad hesitated. Then Ran's second shot whipped past close to his ear, and he hesitated no longer. He dived awkwardly off the ledge, landed in the water with a big belly whop, and began paddling around frantically. Cut off for the moment from Ran's view, he dazedly wondered what the hell he could do next.

The answer came to him fast as he saw Ran appear on the ledge above him, his young face distorted with rage as he again levered the rifle and brought it to bear.

Thad hunched his back and dived deep into the pool. Dimly he heard the roar of Ran's rifle. Then he found himself slamming up against the barrier of boulders that contained the deep pool of the Swimhole. He knew what lay below it

— long stretches of rapids that boiled over partly submerged rocks. But he had no choice.

He flung himself up and over the dam of rocks and slid down into the rapids. At the same time Ran sent another shot that careened off a boulder close to his head.

Then Thad was caught up in the merciless sweep of water.

He thrashed and floundered about wildly in the roiling rapids, but he was a poor swimmer at best. He was caught head over heels as the current bore him downstream, his body smashed against the stony upthrusts, strangling on water that filled his mouth and nose. Desperately he tried to strike for shore. At the same time he knew that if he did, Ran could still draw a bead and maybe improve his aim. So he let himself be swept along.

Now Thad was dimly aware that the river made a sudden bend, which would put him out of Ran's immediate view. He'd have to gamble that Ran wouldn't be inclined to pursue him any farther.

Thad redoubled his efforts to fight free of the mainstream torrent. He tore the ends of his fingers in several attempts to scramble free of the water. Each time he slipped back into the river, and it bore him relentlessly onward.

Finally he succeeded in catching hold of an obstructing rock along the west bank. He clung to it tightly.

Slowly, still choking on water, Thad clawed his way up the crumbled bank, built up from rock and earth that had fallen from the over-hanging cliff, and hauled himself free of the river. He flopped facedown on the narrow margin of ground. For a while he just lay coughing and gasping, trying to get his breath back.

Goddamn that kid! How had he come on the scene at just this time? Maybe he had come to spy on his sister bathing in the nude, Thad thought with a crooked and totally amoral smile.

Laboriously he dragged himself upward. The bare flesh of his legs and feet, as well as his clothed upper body, was scraped and bleeding. Exhaustedly Thad began to make his way down-stream along the narrow shore between the river and the adjoining cliff, seeking a place where he could ascend the escarpment.

He did note in a dim and puzzled way that the rubble under his feet bore the faint tracks of someone who had tramped repeatedly along the same strip of ground. Some of the tracks headed downstream, some upstream. He wondered about that, but not very much.

Ugly and morose, Thad cursed steadily as he limped on. His pants and boots, not to mention his horse, were back by the Swimhole. He would have to recover them somehow. . . .

Then he became suddenly alert. Ahead of him an exceptionally large amount of rubble had crumbled away from above, spilling out into the river. The earth was still fresh; it must have happened recently.

Thad paused, peering up at the overhanging

117

cliff. By God, somebody must have been whacking away up there. *Why?* The scars of the man's diggings showed plainly.

Curious now, Thad dropped to his knees, inspecting the rubble, sifting it through his fingers. He found glimmering particles of metal that looked like gold.

Jesus! That must be it. Someone had been digging the stuff out. Thad's nimble mind needed only a moment's speculation to tell him who it was.

Gage Cameron. Very probably he had come on the gold the same day that Thad and his two cronies had placed enough shots near him to cause him to fall all the way down. Finding a considerable lode of gold at this point, he had been quietly and clandestinely taking it out and conveying it somewhere well away from here.

Quickly and shrewdly Thad further deduced that Cameron had a good reason for being secretive. This place lay within RBJ's boundary line. The breed had no legal right to mine it — so he had taken the gold out illegally.

Despite the misery of his cuts and pains, Thad began to grin as, still squatting on his haunches, he juggled a handful of sparkling dirt in his palm. Almost certainly there was a lot more gold buried in the upper cliff.

Naked greed boiled in his brain.

Why should he share this knowledge with his uncle? Why shouldn't he have the whole gold find for himself? Hell, it should be easy to manage

— once both Gage Cameron and R. B. Janeece were out of the way.

A few hours later, Thad's physical condition was even more miserable. He had followed the river downstream to a place where it shallowed out. There he had forded it to reach the east bank, then had struck out overland toward an RBJ line shack that he knew lay almost due east.

This time he let out only a few cusswords, despite the fact that his bare and bleeding feet and legs were lacerated all over again by stretches of the flint-strewn and thorn-grown terrain he had to cross.

A man with a fortune in his near-grasp could afford to tolerate a few more scratches on his bare hide.

The line shack was occupied by a pair of Mexican wranglers, the Ortez brothers, Gregorio and Julio. Gregorio was apparently out performing his duties on-range. Julio was standing in the doorway, sipping a cup of coffee as he leaned one shoulder against the jamb, his other shoulder quaking with amusement as he watched Thad's staggering approach.

"Ho! You cut a fine figure, Senor Overmile," he said in a pleased voice. "Maybe you tell me wha' happen, eh?"

"Maybe I won't, too," Thad snarled softly. "I tell you what, Hooley. You rummage me up a pair of boots and some pants and loan me a horse. Then keep your mouth shut about this."

Julio grinned, impudently raising a brow. "Well, senor. My brother, he got to know. He is big like you are. Is his spare pants and boots I got to give you."

"That's fine. Then you both keep your mouths shut. If a word of this ever gets out, I'll come back and smash your grinning spick teeth down your throats. *Comprende?*"

Julio's grin faded; his eyes narrowed. "Sure, boss," he said softly.

CHAPTER TWELVE

Opal Bedoe was outside in the yard, washing clothes under a pallid midmorning sun. Altogether, the work was untaxing and almost enjoyable. The weather was pleasantly cool; the faint warmth of sun against her right side was nice, not enough to draw out any sweat. She enjoyed the stretch of the lithe muscles in her back and arms as she knelt by a bench and push-pulled soiled clothes up and down a washboard set in a bucket of soapy water. She wrung out the garments one by one and dropped them in a basket at her side.

Reeve was out back plowing. Now that he'd finished most of the work on his buildings, he wanted to get in a planting of corn and root vegetables for the year. Opal liked the rich bass of his voice throwing out strident urgings to the team. An occasional touch of cursing, too, but he really was trying to curb his language as he'd promised.

Opal arose; smiling a little as she rubbed her lower back, straightening a kink out of it. Then she picked up the basket and carried it to a clothesline rope strung between a pair of tall posts next to the cabin. She shook the wet clothes out and fastened them to the line, holding the clothes-pins a few at a time between her teeth, humming as she worked. Finished, she carried the basket back to the bench, dumped the discolored water out of the bucket, and then brought it to the brook to refill it.

After she'd toted it back to the porch, she went into the cabin to see how baby Ishmael was doing. He was fine, lying on his back in his crib and amusing himself by kicking at the air. Lord! What a jolly little bundle of energy he was, always coo-ing, and (she hoped) not far from saying his first recognizable word. Both she and Reeve were look-ing forward to the day.

She picked him up and hugged him, murmured some silly talk, and laid him carefully back in his crib.

Opal went back outside, knelt by the bench, and worked up a good suds in the bucket from her crude bar of homemade lye soap. She began to dunk more dirty garments and rasp them along the washboard. She wore a faint, pleased smile, humming softly as she worked.

Opal flung her head up suddenly and quit scrubbing.

A couple of riders had come off the timbered height to the east. Uneasily she watched their steady approach. Lord . . . this was as it had been on two occasions before. Opal stood up and called "Reeve!" as she dried her hands on her skirt.

She heard Reeve shout the team to a halt. In

122

a few moments he came around the cabin at a half run, rifle in his hands. He always kept it nearby now, even lashing it to the cross beam of his plow.

He hauled up at Opal's side. "Better go inside, honeybunch," he said, looking at her from the corners of his eyes.

Opal glanced at him sharply, then shook her head. He said no more but moved out a few steps ahead of her.

They waited in silence as the two horsemen pulled up several yards away. They were Thad Overmile and a thick-bodied Indian, a full-blood, she guessed. Both men were armed with pistols and rifles but had left their weapons sheathed.

Opal felt mingled anger and despair ferment in her stomach. Lord, she thought. What are they about?

Reeve said quietly, "Gentlemen. What do you want now?" He held the rifle half-raised as he shifted his weight from one foot to the other.

"Depends," Thad said, crossing his arms on his pommel in an easy, negligent way.

"On what?"

"What we find here. We heard talk, Uncle. So I came to investigate."

Reeve continued to sway back and forth on his feet, ominously. "You got one half a minute to state your full business. Then you get the hell out of here."

"All right, all right —" Thad raised a hand

placatingly. "A rider of ours was out. He came on track beyond the ridge yonder. Signs show that a jag of our cows got driven off and pointed this way. He came to tell us."

"Yeah?" Reeve's heavy jaw ridged out tightly. "So?"

"Well, you wouldn't mind us giving your place a lookover, would you?"

"Hell, yes, man, I damn well do mind! What you expect to find? You see any cattle here? You see any cattle track around my place?"

"No." Thad thumb-nudged his hat back on his head with a mildly perplexed scowl. "I have to allow that much. Now Pokey here —" he pointed the thumb at his Indian companion "— he's a Pima. They're the best damn trackers in the world. He couldn't find anything this side of that ridge. But the thing is, you see, someone might have driven our cows off elsewhere. Or . . . they might be butchered and hanging up in yonder shed." He nodded at the nearly finished barn. "That is, if —"

"Get out." Reeve said it flatly and tonelessly, tipping the rifle up.

"Jesus, take it easy. All I asked was, could I have a look?"

"You got your answer. Didn't bring any law along this time, did you?"

"None," Thad said affably. "Looks like you're holding all the authority in your fists. Be a neighborly gesture on your part, though."

" 'Neighborly'?" Reeve stared at him incredulously. He glanced at Pokey's ugly and inexpressive face, then back at Thad Overmile. "What the hell you up to, man?"

Opal had been wondering the same thing. The discussion seemed senseless. It didn't get anywhere, and Overmile must have known it wouldn't. What was he driving at?

Now Thad was looking almost injured. "Look, all right, we've had our differences. We don't need any more. If we did, I could have ridden in with more men at my back, couldn't I? I mean it, Bedoe, I —"

"So do I," Reeve said between his clenched teeth. "Get out, the both of you. Now."

As he spoke, he ceased to shift his feet about and froze in place, his thumb tensing on the rifle's hammer.

That was when the sullen boom of a distant shot came.

Reeve jerked around with the bullet's impact. His jaw hung open, and his eyes met Opal's with a terrible fixity. She saw a red patch spring across the side of his shirt.

She was aware of a gray bloom of powder smoke from the deep brush a short way up the wooded ridge. And she saw Reeve buckle slowly at the middle and pitch forward on his face.

Opal stood frozen, the beginning of a scream stuck in her throat. She stared at the two riders. They looked unsurprised and totally unconcerned. Then the wildness of a cornered tigress galvanized her into action. Her husband had

125

fallen on his rifle; it was partly pinned beneath his body.

She bent down and tried to wrench it free.

Thad's voice, soft and amused, penetrated the fog of her rage. "Let it go, pretty. Or I'll have to open up your sweet black hide, too."

Opal saw the pistol in his hand. Slowly she straightened up, facing him. "Stand away," Thad told her, and then swung out of his saddle to the ground.

She didn't move. Thad walked over to her and clouted her backhand across the jaw. She stumbled back a few steps, then dropped to her knees. As dazed as she was, red lights popping in her vision, she realized that Reeve had gotten his hands under him and was pushing himself doggedly to his knees, his eyes varnished with the befuddled shock of his wound.

No, no, no . . .

Opal tried to articulate the relentless refrain pounding in her brain into speech. For Thad was aiming his pistol, holding it out at arm's length, pointing it at Reeve.

The man who had fired from the ridge had scrambled down to its base by now and was coming forward on the trot. He was carrying what she vaguely recognized as a big Sharps buffalo gun. It was the man for hire called Breck. He had brought Reeve down with the Sharps. He'd only been waiting for the moment when Reeve was a stationary target.

Breck hauled up by Thad Overmile, who said

casually, "We got us a treed coon here. Good shooting. You want a piece of this? Help put him out of his plight?"

"No reason why not," Breck murmured.

He tucked the Sharps under his left arm and pulled his six-gun with his right hand. "You go ahead," Breck said with a still-faced courtesy. He might have been commenting on the weather.

Thad cocked his pistol and shot Reeve in the stomach just as the black man succeeded in pushing himself up onto his knees. The slug slammed Reeve over backward.

Breck said, "Good shooting yourself," and fired his bullet into Reeve's face.

Opal's voice found release in a scream.

She watched the two men fire shot after shot, until their guns were empty, into Reeve's heaving body until it subsided into twitchings, and then lay silent and mutilated. His clothes were covered with blood, and some of it had spattered onto her skirt.

That was her last fleeting thought before her shocked brain went totally blank and she slipped away into darkness. . . .

Opal revived slowly. She became hazily aware, lying on her back on the damp earth, that a team and wagon had been pulled up in the yard close to the barn.

The wagon was laden with what appeared to be the raw carcasses of skinned and half-butchered steers. The attention of the three men — Thad

127

Overmile, the gunman Breck, and the Pima called Pokey — was off her as they proceeded to unload the steer carcasses from the wagon and carry them into the barn.

She had a vague and horrified realization of what they were likely up to, but even that thought was submerged in the instant worry for her infant son in the cabin. He was quiet now, and she supposed that the rattle of gunfire had shocked him into silence.

They won't hurt him. Not a baby.

But what about her? She was a witness to what they had done and were doing. Why should they leave a witness? And she was dead sure that Thad Overmile, at least, had other plans for her. She had never sensed such transparent lust in a man, today or in the previous times the RBJ men had invaded the place.

Opal forced herself to cast one glance toward the bloody ruin of her husband's sprawled body and did not look at him again.

She wasn't sure that she wanted to live any longer. Nearly all her world had been wiped out with Reeve's death. All except baby Ishmael. As long as she still lived, she had to stay alive. For him.

Her mind was functioning quite clearly now, calculating. She awaited her chance, playing possum. With muscles gathered and tense, she watched for a few moments until she could be sure that all three men were in the barn at the same time.

Then she sprang to her feet and began to run, heading for a patch of uncleared brush off to the west of the headquarters. She reached it and pushed deep inside it, then shrank down on her haunches, heart pounding. She was cut off from direct view of the buildings now but was well hidden enough, at least for a time. If they came looking for her, she could swiftly fade back into deeper brush, eluding them until nightfall.

Opal's jaw ached cruelly where Overmile had struck her, but that was of minor concern. What she had to do, she would do. Somehow . . .

And then, quite suddenly, she saw an eruption of smoke from the headquarters, a gray column unfurling slowly in the sky. *God.* They had set something afire. Could it be the cabin?

Oh God, no. They wouldn't!

But only blind, unthinking instinct dominated her mind now. *Ishmael!* She plowed free of the brush and started back at a run for the buildings.

Coming in sight of them, she let out a wailing cry. Yes. They had fired the cabin.

Too late, she realized that it must have been the men's intent to draw her out. For even as she broke into the open, she saw the three advancing in her direction, guns out, spread far enough apart that they couldn't fail to see her if she showed herself. Maybe it had been a mere guess on their part, but it had worked.

Opal halted. She hesitated a long moment, hands fisted at her sides. Then, caught in the blind terror of the moment, she whirled about and raced back for the brush.

At once the men opened fire. That was her answer. She was as good as dead. . . .

She reached the edge of the brushy cover when a bullet struck her in the head. Blood showered her face. She kept running. She reached the brushy cover again before her mind blacked out once more, this time in a flare of bursting pain.

CHAPTER THIRTEEN

Gage Cameron was out on one of his solitary prowls through the wooded region southwest of his family's headquarters, looking for some likely game, when he heard the distant reports of gunshots from the west. He cocked his head, listening intently.

Could Reeve Bedoe be having more trouble? Most likely not, although it was the first thought that sprang to his mind. Probably just some stray hunter like himself, out game seeking.

The shooting had subsided quickly. Gage listened a while longer, then shook his head. Whatever the stir of gunfire had been about, it was over. He might as well pursue his usual pastime.

Within the next couple of hours, he had a chance to bring down a big mule-deer buck, and he spent some time skinning and butchering it out and then tying the usable meat and hide to his packhorse. He was pleased. This kill would take care of his family's needs for table meat for a couple of months.

At the same time, however, a twinge of conscience kept nagging him. Damn. Maybe he should have gone at once to check on the source of that faraway gunfire. He had a feeling of ob-

131

ligation to the black couple, Reeve and Opal.

Abruptly Gage made his decision. He turned his mount westward and, leading the packhorse, headed for the Bedoe place.

Well before he reached it, he saw a gray plume of smoke spiraling up from beyond the east ridge that bordered on the Bedoe homestead claim. He felt a thickening dread in his throat and quickened his pace.

When Gage came over the timbered ridge, he saw that his initial fear hadn't been wrong. The Bedoes' cabin had been set afire; already it was largely consumed by a seething swirl of flames.

Gage rode down quickly to the site and piled off his horse as near to the cabin as he could stand the heat. He stood immobile for a few moments, trying to digest with a sickened shock as much as he could tell of what had happened.

Reeve Bedoe's body lay sprawled in the yard, shot almost to pieces. But what of Opal and the baby? Had they been caught inside the burning cabin? If they had, there was no help for them now.

Shaking himself back to his senses, Gage began to reconnoiter the ground, studying it with all his woodsman's lore. He could spell out some of what had occurred . . . at least in part.

The riders had approached the place from the east, coming across the timbered ridge. Somehow they had managed to kill Reeve. He wouldn't easily be taken, after he had given vow to keep his rifle close to him always. The rifle wasn't anywhere near his body, though. And another man had come off the ridge on foot to this spot. Still unable to be sure what he might deduce from this meager evidence, Gage did some more figuring.

He found the butchered bodies of four steers in the barn, hung up (presumably) for cooling and seasoning. They had been skinned out and the hides slung carelessly into a corner. Gage examined the skins carefully. The brands on them showed every sign of having been worked over. They had been "vent-branded," the brands being crudely faked from the conventional RBJ brand to an RB . . . no doubt to stand for Reeve Bedoe.

It was about as clumsy a job of brand forging as one could imagine. But any white man's court that passed judgment on it wouldn't be long deciding on the verdict against Reeve Bedoe: *guilty.*

Not that it would matter to Bedoe himself; he was dead. But it would validate whatever act had been committed against him to a white judge or jury.

Feeling sick in his guts, a way he was getting more and more used to feeling, Gage Cameron continued to scan the ground patiently. He began to piece together, in odd fragments, what else must have happened.

Opal Bedoe, whose light, slim shoe prints he could easily identify, had somehow gotten away from the invaders. She had stumbled out into some uncleared brush terrain nearby, and the men had gone after her. They had shot at and hit her; he saw splatters of blood on the earth. Now, following the track, Gage swiftly found where they had overtaken her.

Opal lay on her back in a tangle of brush, and her whole head was covered with congealing blood. She must have bled terribly. Yet bending down close to her now, Gage was astonished to hear her faint, shallow breathing. She was still alive. Not too surprising at that; any wound in the scalp would bleed copiously.

But those men must have left her for dead. They wouldn't want to leave any live witnesses to what had happened.

Gage carried Opal Bedoe out of the brush and laid her on her back in a cleared patch of ground away from the dying embers of the cabin. Then he fetched his saddle horse and packhorse to the spot. He threw the gear and butchered meat off both animals and ground-tethered them nearby after watering them at the stream.

Afterward he tended to Opal, building a small fire and boiling up a pan of water. He cleaned her head wound and found that despite its fatal appearance it was quite superficial. Little more than a crease on the scalp, the bullet must have angled against her skull with a vicious force before glancing off.

Gage put on a crude bandage and then covered her with a couple of blankets from his own gear.

By now the hour was close to evening, and

Gage was feeling worn-down, more from pure depression (and maybe a touch of self-blame for not coming sooner) than from anything else. He sat by the tiny fire and pulled up his knees, settled his chin on them, and quickly went to sleep.

He woke suddenly. Opal was letting out soft moans; she seemed to be partly awake but was also half-feverish. She had pulled her arms from under the blankets and was feebly scrabbling her hands at the air, her head thrashing slowly from side to side.

Gage rose stiffly, went over to her, and tried to soothe her, speaking softly. Finally she did seem to relax, drifting off again.

Gage lay down and dozed a little more. He was brought out of a light sleep by Opal's low murmur: "Mr. Cameron . . . ?"

She was fully awake, her head turned toward him. But her voice held to a dead and incurious level. The baby, he thought. She knows.

By now it was completely dark. The night was clear, the sky riddled with stars. The fire had died to glowing coals. Gage stood up, pulling his numb muscles into motion. He tossed more fuel on the fire. As it blazed up, he went over to Opal and crouched beside her.

"How are you feeling?"

"Alive, I suppose," she said listlessly, tonelessly, and turned her gaze away from him. "Unless this is hell and I'm already in some kind of . . . what, afterlife?"

"I don't believe that's the case, ma'am."

Carefully he told her how he'd come to be here and what he had found, and what he judged about the whole matter. The woman did not look at him again, nor did she say a word through his whole recitation. She simply stared upward, her face utterly dead to expression.

She remained silent for a full minute after Gage ceased speaking. He stayed in his awkward crouch and was almost ready to speak up again when Opal spoke first, very softly.

"I'm going to kill them, Mr. Cameron. The men who did this. I am going to kill all three of them."

Gage didn't know how to reply. He tried instead to gently draw her out on just what had happened. Opal replied to his queries in the same dead and toneless manner, and she never once looked up at him, but just stared skyward.

Her story filled in the few remaining gaps. As Gage had already assumed, Reeve Bedoe's murder had been covered by implicating him for rustling RBJ stock; that Reeve had been a black man would make the frame-up almost a surefire cinch. More obliquely, it would serve as a warning to other homesteading folk who attempted to settle the vast graze of these public-domain lands.

People like R. B. Janeece and his nephew Thad fought the tide of history. But then so had a lot of others. The dust of time would blow over the bones of their ambitions. Maybe they knew

136

it and didn't give a damn so long as they could get what they wanted here and now, in their own lifetimes.

Human beings are a lot of bastards, Gage thought obscurely. And you're no better than any of them, you greedy, lazy son of a bitch.

In the back of his mind he knew that was partly true, partly nonsense. Most people possessed enough virtues to at least balance out their faults. But in the leaden and abject disgust he experienced just now, it was hard to feel any other way.

Opal spoke again, gently, and now she was looking straight at him. "Did you hear me before, Mr. Cameron? I am going to kill those men."

"I heard you." Gage shifted uneasily on his haunches. "But you're in no shape to undertake anything of the sort."

"I will be. Give me a few days to get better. Then I'll do it."

"How? Have you thought about that?"

"No. But I'll have the time to think of something."

"Not if you stay here, you won't."

Her eyes half questioned him, and then she stirred her bandaged head in a painful nod. "I understand. Now that they have blamed the Bedoes for stealing their cattle, they will have official lawmen on a search for stolen stock. And they will find the carcasses here."

"Yes. And there's a chance you'll go to prison,

ma'am, if they do."

Opal blinked her eyes; she hesitated. "I hate to ask. But could you. . . ?"

"Take you somewhere? Hide you out?"

"Yes."

Gage nodded slowly. "And cover our tracks so they can't follow us."

"Yes."

He met her gaze squarely. "Mrs. Bedoe, what about the bodies? Do you want me to bury them? Your husband and your baby?"

"Why?" Opal said matter-of-factly. "If they find fresh-turned earth, wouldn't they just dig them up to determine their identities?"

Gage scrubbed a fist along his jaw. "I'm afraid that's so."

"They're dead now. So what does it matter? Those men will bury them anyway. I'd assume they'd have that much decency. Although I can't be sure. They burned down the cabin with my baby inside it . . . and I'd never have dreamed they would do anything like that." A long, shuddering sigh left her. "God!"

Gage cleared his throat. "Ma'am, could be they didn't know about your baby inside."

"Oh . . . that's possible, I suppose. But look at how they killed Reeve. As if they were literally shooting him to bits. Men like that might do anything!"

"Maybe the Indian didn't know. The sign I found showed that only Overmile and Breck were the ones who killed your husband."

"Does it matter? *My baby is just as dead!*"

"Yes'm."

"And if they knew what they were doing, the Pima, or whatever he is, made no move to stop them. *Did he?*"

"Hard to tell. I didn't find any sign that would indicate as much."

"Very well. *Then?*"

Gage stood up, shaking a few cramps out of his muscles. "I'll get you out of here. At first light tomorrow. Meantime try to rest all you can. I need some sleep myself. It'll be a ways from here . . . the place I'm taking you to."

CHAPTER FOURTEEN

Thad Overmile sat in the office of the main house at RBJ headquarters. He was slacked in his uncle's swivel chair next to the desk, his legs crossed and boots propped atop the desk, mildly scowling as he pared his fingernails with the small blade of his pocketknife.

Hurd Tancred stood hulking in the doorway, giving Thad about as much hell as he might have expected. "Jesus," Hurd rumbled. "What a damn dumb thing to do! You lose all your wits or what?"

Thad glanced up, saying irritably, "It was one of your big ideas, remember? I just followed through on it."

"You sure as hell did. It's *how* you done it that gravels me. Jesus! You could've managed it without shooting that nigger all to hell and gone. Then trying to do for his wife. And his baby. Jesus!"

"You don't really give a damn, Hurd," Thad said insolently, smiling a little.

"That ain't the point. But God. The *baby!*"

"Look, we didn't know about any baby inside the cabin. Not till we looked it over when we came back." Impatiently Thad swung his feet to the floor. "What's done is done. No point weeping

140

alligator tears over it."

Tancred, his thick face filled with disgust, eyed him a few moments longer. "Maybe not. But your uncle left orders you was to consult me 'fore any move was made."

"All right. I didn't. And now it's done. What do you plan to do about it, Hurd?"

Tancred rammed his hands into his hip pockets. He paced the length of the office and then swung back to the doorway. "Not a goddamned thing," he said heavily. "Nothing I can do and get what I want out of all this. You had that figured."

"Well, certainly."

"What I don't understand is why you had to do what you done in such a plain damn murderous way. You could've overcome them Bedoes some other way, left 'em knocked out or whatever. . . ."

"No," Thad said patiently. "Look, you're so damned bright. Once we did the job, Breck and Pokey and me, we could leave 'em knocked out, and by the time we fetched the law, they'd be up and around again and might even have got those butchered cows out of sight, somewhere or other. You follow me so far?"

Tancred eyed him as if he were looking at a crazy man. Maybe he was, Thad thought, barely suppressing the urge to chuckle out loud.

Immediately after Thad and Breck had committed the atrocity at Reeve Bedoe's place, they had ridden with Pokey to Glade and asked Deputy Sheriff Manly Jackson, who policed this remote pocket of the county, to accompany them back to Bedoe's claim.

The story they gave Jackson was that Pokey had discovered that some RBJ steers had been driven off in that direction. When they had followed up this lead, Reeve Bedoe had refused to let them look the place over in search of the steers. Unexpectedly he had gotten desperate and had pulled down on them with his rifle. They'd been forced to shoot him. His wife had grabbed up the rifle and run away, trying to escape in the nearby brush. They had caught up with her and had urged her to surrender, but her only reply had been to turn the rifle on them, and they'd been forced to shoot her.

Altogether it was a pretty feeble-sounding story, but it would do for Jackson, who had accompanied them on the previous visit to Bedoe's claim, and it would do for most of the white citizens of this county. Also, Pokey the Pima had verified everything he'd been told to say, and he (as a full-blooded Indian tracker) would be believed.

However, a few things had happened that they hadn't counted on. Opal Bedoe's body was gone from where they had left it, deep in the brush. Reeve Bedoe's horses had been unhitched from the plow and turned loose. Also, his barn had been burned up, much as Thad himself had ordered the main house set afire. The butchered steers inside the barn were charred beyond recognition.

Someone else had fired the barn, maybe the

same party who had turned the horses loose and taken Opal's body away. That much seemed pretty obvious. But who had done it? Thad's first suspicion had pounced on Gage Cameron. That goddamned half-breed had been a thorn in his side from the first, and he'd shown a special sympathy for those Bedoe niggers. Yet why would Cameron have removed Opal from the spot . . . *unless she was still alive?*

The possibility gnawed at Thad. He could have sworn she'd been shot dead. But he hadn't made sure. If she was still living, it might throw his own plans into jeopardy.

Tancred was still watching him guardedly. Thad smiled and held out both hands, palms up. "What else can I say, Hurd?"

"Nothing, I reckon. But I know one damn thing, fella."

"What's that?"

"You and Breck didn't need to shoot the nigger up the way you done. You must've enjoyed doing it."

"Why, yes. Anything else?"

The hour was nearly midnight. Light from the lamp on the desk shed a sallow glow through the office. It painted both men with an odd, flickering light that, Thad guessed, must make them look almost ghoulish in each other's eyes. To him, Hurd surely did.

Tancred had been out on-range attending to his usual duties, and he and the other crewmen had gotten in late this evening. Thad had taken him aside and told him everything. Correction — *almost* everything.

Hurd had been angry as hell, but he was already starting to simmer down, as Thad had expected he would. Resigned acceptance had settled into the foreman's manner.

"All right," Tancred said tiredly. "But God. That baby."

"Forget it," Thad said flatly. "I told you before. What's done is done. I didn't mean for it to happen, but it did."

That was true enough. Setting fire to the cabin, he and Breck hadn't known about the baby inside. At the same time, Thad knew, the knowledge might not have prevented them from doing it. He admitted as much to himself, as well as the fact that he really couldn't care less. But he would need Hurd Tancred's assistance to carry through what else he had in mind.

Now was the time to strike, while the iron was hot.

Thad laced the fingers of both hands together and leaned forward in his chair, setting his elbows on his knees. "Hurd, I want to confide in you. Let's forget about this Bedoe business. You and I can both be rich men. What I'm about to tell you should put us squarely in the same corner, if anything can."

Tancred eyed him cautiously. "Yeah? What's that?"

"Just listen. . . ."

144

CHAPTER FIFTEEN

Gage Cameron had taken Opal Bedoe up into higher country, to a spot about two miles from the Bedoe homestead claim and an equal distance to the west of his own family's headquarters.

Before he left the Bedoe claim, Gage set fire to the barn containing the steer carcasses. He also disengaged Reeve's two team horses from the plow and turned them loose. He hoped it would help disconcert any lawmen that Thad and Breck and their Pima tracker would later bring to inspect the place. Let Thad explain that. Let him also explain what might have happened to Opal, whom he had apparently left for dead.

He transported Opal on an improvised travois fastened behind his packhorse, which also bore the chunks of a butchered deer tied onto it. The dragged ends of the travois would leave a plain track for anyone to follow, and Gage worried some about that. But he had already detected the signs of a storm brewing. The sky had a dirty, clouded look, and it indicated that heavy rain was coming. The storm would wipe out any trail left by the travois.

The rain did unleash itself late in the day, pouring down relentlessly as Gage pressed northward.

At about sunset he reached his destination, a rocky outcrop that formed a sturdy overhang and provided a sort of shallow cave underneath. Below that lay an open and brush-free incline, and Gage would have a clear view of anyone who attempted to steal up on them. Meantime it would give Opal a place where she'd be shielded from the weather.

They were soaking wet, and Opal was running a quiet fever by the time they reached the scanty cover. It was nearly dark, and rain had slacked off to a light downpour. Gage looked over their back trail and was satisfied that the storm had completely wiped out the sign, leaving nothing that Overmile's Pima tracker could pick up.

Gage got Opal under the sheltering rock and out of the wet. Then he unslung his gear and the quarters of butchered buck from the horses and hauled them under the outcrop, too. Afterward he tethered the horses in a nearby grove where plenty of grass grew between the trees beside a small, rustling stream; then he grained them.

Returning to the shallow cave, he built a fire from the dry brush that laced the underside of the outcrop. Opal was writhing with fever. He wrapped her in a couple of dry wool blankets that had escaped soaking under a tarp.

By now Gage was as hungry as hell. He cooked up a sizable portion of the deer meat and gobbled it down.

Opal was still twisting in her fever, mumbling

incoherently. God. What a horrible situation for her. Behind the outward calm she had shown him before, she must be nearly deranged with grief.

Gage did what he could to make her comfortable.

The venison would supply them with food for quite a while, and he could supplement it with wild onions and tubers and berries. He could also cook up some of the meat to produce a broth that he could spoon into her while she made a slow recovery.

Meantime he could sit up with her all night. And he did.

For the next few days Opal tossed off and on in fever. Gage was convinced that it was caused less by her head wound than by the wiping out of her whole life — her husband and baby.

Yet now and then she would have lucid intervals when they would talk.

Gage told her about his gold find and what it might mean to his family, and how he'd tried to keep the discovery secret. He also told her about the deserted Navaho village above the cliff and the apparently supernatural manifestations that had occurred.

He said: "Reckon that last must sound pretty foolish, eh?"

"It doesn't, Mr. Cameron," Opal murmured. "My race has its superstitions, too. So do the whites, except that they call it their religion."

"So do we."

"True. My grandfather once told me that our stock is of the Ushanti tribe . . . and we had our share. I've never believed in any of it. Or just wasn't sure, up till now. You seem very convinced."

"Maybe I am."

Yet no matter what they spoke about, it would circle back to Opal's calm determination to kill Thad Overmile. Nothing he said could dissuade her. The woman's deadly goal hadn't lessened by a jot. If anything, it grew more fixed and unyielding.

"I'm going to kill those men, Mr. Cameron. I am going to kill all of them."

Gage said wearily, "Yeah. You've said that before. But damned if I know how you'll go about it."

"There'll be a way," Opal said confidently, staring at the rock overhang above.

It was evening of the third day they had spent together. Opal was still weak and dizzy, but her strength was coming back fast, thanks to Gage's constant ministrations. She was much better physically, but her single-minded fixation on getting back at the RBJ crowd was more rooted than ever.

"You'll have to go onto their property, Mrs. Bedoe," Gage said in the usual mechanical way. "You'll have to find each one and dispose of him. I don't think you'll make it. Not a very practical procedure."

Opal glanced sidelong at him from the blankets on which she lay, and surprisingly she smiled; "Can't I be, 'Opal' from now on? I think we've been 'Mr.' and 'Mrs.' long enough."

"If you like." He felt a small lift of hope. Could she be coming out of her insensate set of mind at last? "And I'm Gage. But don't you think. . . ?"

"I don't feel any differently. I'm going to —"

"I know, I know," he reiterated tiredly. "I don't blame you. I just don't see how you're going to manage it."

"Perhaps I can," she murmured, and added obliquely, "Perhaps *we* can."

Oh, Christ, Gage thought resignedly. Maybe he had known it would come to this, finally. She would expect to start looking to him for assistance.

Don't get too involved with other people, even inside your own family. That had always been his guiding principle. But he *was* involved, like it or not. With his own family, and with this black woman, who had exerted a strong hold on him from the moment of their first meeting.

Opal knew it, too. And now she was using the knowledge. Like a weapon.

"And how do you propose we do that, ma'am — Opal?" he asked with only a mild irony.

"You know this country. You must know how to make an approach onto the RBJ headquarters. You can find ways to get to each of those men.

Need I make it any plainer?"

"No. It's just that I don't like being used."

"Am I doing that to you?"

"I reckon you are. And you damned well know it."

Opal sighed and shut her eyes, settling one slim arm across them. Then she lifted her hand and looked directly at him again. "Yes. But I don't believe that you'd let a woman go alone against that crew . . . especially not if you had any feeling for her."

"I expect not," Gage said woodenly. "But don't try to turn it into a game — woman against man."

"All right. We're both educated people, you and I, educated in the ways of the whites, I mean. It could be we're even semisophisticates." A corner of her mouth lifted. "Perhaps that's not such a good thing."

"And maybe not altogether bad, either."

"Not from my viewpoint, no."

"Not if you can get what you want, eh?"

"Yes. That's right. Is that completely honest enough for you?"

Gage moodily plucked at a chunk of turf between his feet, shredding the grass and the grainy dirt between his fingers. "Very well," he said abruptly, almost impersonally. "I'll help you . . . in the way you've suggested. It will take some planning ahead."

"Thank you. Yes, it will. Are you sure we should wait?"

"You'll need to rest a couple of days longer anyway," Gage said roughly. "Till all your fever is sweated out."

"Of course. And that will give us time to plan, won't it?" Opal's voice was shaded to a rich, midnight velvet, and he thought: She's still sparring with my feelings.

But who the hell could blame her? She no longer cared about her life, only about whatever fulfillment revenge might give her. Even if he tried to restrain her forcibly now, she would likely be willing to wait for months, even years, until she could finally get a full measure of vengeance. He could *feel* that strength of will in her.

"Yes," Gage said in a somewhat haggard tone. "Just one thing. We can work out how it's to be done between us. But in the end it will have to be *my* decision — only mine — as to what course we follow."

"Of course," Opal said with a kind of mock meekness. "Of course it will be, Gage."

By the time three more days had passed, Opal was back on her feet, actively aiding in camp chores — and surprisingly enough, she seemed half-cheerful. She was fully healed, even mentally, except for her seething desire for revenge. Gage dourly judged that her improved state of mind derived chiefly from her expectation of fulfilling that intention, even if she died in the attempt.

In that case, he was almost certain to die, too. But he had cast his lot, he had committed himself,

and he was stoically prepared for any conse-
quences.

Hell, everyone had to die sometime . . . eventually. Maybe he was a damned fool, but he liked
being his own kind of fool. And he supposed
he was more than halfway in love with Opal
Bedoe. He'd never felt nearly this strongly about
any woman. Gage was a born fatalist. If that's
how it was, that's how it was.

By now his family might be somewhat concerned about his prolonged absence, but he
guessed not very much. Before this, he had been
gone for days at a time and hadn't bothered to
show up at the home hearth until it suited him.

"We can set out tonight," he told Opal on the
afternoon of the third day. "I reckon you're as
fit as you'll ever be."

"Thank you, Gage," she said gravely, and laid
a hand on his arm. "I'm sorry for this . . . for
what it may mean in your life."

Or death, Gage thought, but didn't say the
thought out loud. "Sure. Just one thing. I have
a spare outfit in my plunder. Shirt, pants, boots.
You'd better change into them. We'll have to
move quickly and cautiously at the same time,
and that dress — what's left of it — and your
shoes won't serve you very well."

Opal almost laughed; it came out a sort of spare
chuckle. "Anyway, we're close to the same size.
I'm pretty nearly as tall as you."

Gage smiled grudgingly. "So you are. Though
there might be a few other notable differences."

152

CHAPTER SIXTEEN

During the past three days, Gage had had plenty of time to figure out the best way they could get into RBJ headquarters and accomplish Opal's design. He'd considered everything he knew about the ranch layout, shared it with her, and had drawn diagrams of the place on smoothed-out patches of earth, explaining them to her in painstaking detail.

They were as ready to go ahead as they'd ever be.

Leaving most of their spare gear cached at the campsite, they mounted two of the horses and, before sunset, rode away toward RBJ headquarters It would be after dark when they reached it.

A steady wind had begun to blow, riffling the prairie grass, as they approached the headquarters. From a distance they could see the squares of window light in two buildings, the main house and the bunkhouse.

There was a not-too-isolated copse of trees where they ground-tied the horses. It would be foolhardy to approach any closer to the headquarters, and it might be suicidal to leave the horses any farther away . . . assuming their riders survived to make a running getaway.

Both of them slipped their rifles out of their saddle scabbards. Gage led the way toward the buildings.

He moved slowly and warily, ready for anything. Thad or his uncle might have guards stationed in concealment almost anywhere. By now they would be aware that Opal was alive and that someone had assisted her. No doubt their first suspicion would fix on Gage Cameron. They couldn't be sure that any reprisal might be in the offing on their own ground, but they surely wouldn't discount the possibility.

Gage chose a somewhat circuitous route, hugging the flanks of shallow rises wherever he could. Both he and Opal stayed in low-bent crouches as they moved. The sky was largely clouded over, only a few glimmers of starlight showing.

It took most of an hour to get up to within a hundred feet of the buildings, but in that time nobody challenged them. Gage's main concern was that a ranch dog might pick them up, if there was one. A woodswise man might work around human guards most of the time, but there was no way of avoiding any alarm raised by an alert dog.

The steadily blowing wind might be of some help. All the same, Gage had flatly told Opal that if they were challenged by either dog or a guard before they reached their objective, they were to retreat at once. She hadn't replied directly to that, and he'd chosen to reply to her lack of response as a bleak assent.

"All right," he told her softly as they paused behind a fringe of brush. "That's the main house on the slope just ahead. It's set off a ways from the other buildings. We'll get up next to it and have a look-see through the windows."

Tensed for the bark of a dog, they moved onward and upward in stealthy silence.

They came up by one corner of the house and moved along the wall, pausing here and there to peer through the windows. Not all the rooms were lit; the ones that were showed an attractive and very active Mexican housekeeper bustling from one room to another, at some cleaning-up activities.

They skirted one end of the long building where no windows were lit and came to a patio that was boxed in by tall and neatly trimmed juniper hedges. Gage pushed noiselessly through a hedge, holding the branches spread open for Opal as she followed him.

Now they were standing inside the patio, which was broadly illumined by a blaze of lamplight from inside. The patio fronted on a pair of French doors.

It was not going to be easy, Gage thought. But they had come this far unhindered. He sidled up to the French doors and looked inside.

There they were, both Thad Overmile and Hurd Tancred, in a lavish parlor. Both men were slacked in stuffed, upholstered armchairs, smoking and drinking and talking. He could make out the muted drift of their voices, but not the words.

"Here's our chance," he murmured to Opal as he half raised his rifle. "We do it now or never. Which one do you want?"

"You know," she snarled. *"Overmile."*

"And I'll take Tancred. For God's sake, make your shot good. Then we clear out of here. As fast as we can."

"There's still that Breck. And the Pima —"

"Will you forget about them! We'll be damned lucky if we can bring off this much —"

"That's no lie, you son of an Injun," Breck's mildly amused voice drawled, suddenly and so close to them that both froze in place with their rifles lifted almost shoulder level.

"We're right here, old son," Breck added. "Four of us. You twitch an eyelash and you get riddled seven ways from sundown. You and that nigra wench both."

It was no bluff. Through the screening hedges now, Gage could see the gleam of light on gun barrels. He felt a rush of chagrin at being surprised so easily.

"You must have had this pretty well figured out," he said quietly.

"We did," Breck said pleasantly. "We been posted in close to the house five nights now, and each night Mr. Overmile and Mr. Tancred been sitting in there palavering, right out in plain sight o' this patio here. Weren't sure you'd try anything of the sort, but no use taking chances. Huh?"

"All right," Gage said. "Now what?"

"You'll find out the most of it soon enough. Mr. Overmile will sing the tune, you listen. Right now we want for you to drop your cannons. Just drop 'em."

Gage looked at Opal, waiting, hoping to God she wouldn't try anything foolish. With no hint of expression, she let the rifle clatter to the stones at her feet. Gage did the same.

Breck and his men pushed through the hedges onto the patio. They were as wolfish-looking a crew of hardcases as Gage had ever seen.

Breck motioned one of the men to pick up the rifles, while he and the others kept their guns trained on Gage and Opal.

"Neatly done," Gage said. "I wouldn't have believed it of you."

"That's your trouble." Breck grinned. "You didn't. That's why you got caught like rats in a trap. Nearly always pays a man to be *too* careful, huh? Now you both stand like you are whilst we inspect you for any more hardware you might have hid on you."

It was a thorough inspection, and the toughs were particularly thorough in patting Opal over. They turned up a revolver and knife on each, as well as a particular blade that Gage always kept strapped in a sheath by his right calf under his pants.

It had been his ace in the hole if he'd ever needed one. Loss of it made him feel almost naked.

By now Thad Overmile and Hurd Tancred had seen what was going on outside. Thad came to the French doors and opened them, motioning everyone to come inside.

"You always do a pretty fair job, Breck," he observed, closing the doors behind them.

"That's what you pay me for."

"And very handsomely. Keep the guns on them, fellows. And a sharp watch, too."

Thad moved around the group and over to a liquor cabinet from which he took a decanter and three glasses. He filled the glasses and handed one apiece to Hurd Tancred and Breck. The third he took himself, draining off half its contents in a gulp.

"Well," he said, letting out his breath with a whoosh. "I guess we three can certainly stand one of these . . . now." He glanced at Gage. "You've given us some tense hours, Charlie, waiting on you these nights."

Gage swiveled a glance around the room, noting the trophy heads that decorated every wall. He looked back at Thad, saying coldly, "The name's Gage Cameron."

"I know. It ought to be Injun Charlie." Thad finished his drink. "We suspected, after considering all possibilities, that you and your black chum here might try something at close quarters. But we out-Injuned you, it seems."

"Get to the point," Gage said flatly. "You intend something particular for us. Or your hired poodles could have cut us down right off."

"Of course." Thad was already mellowing toward near geniality. He poured himself another drink and ran an admiring gaze over Opal, who stared back at him stonily. "Very sightly creature, that. I do admire your taste, breed. Well, it's this way. Breck and the boys will take you two up in the hills where Uncle Bob Janeece is hunting. That's about all he does, or cares to do, as a glance at the wall ornaments must have shown you. Meanwhile Mr. Tancred and I have other fish to fry —"

"Don't tell him!" Tancred growled quickly. "He's still alive, ain't he?"

"Not for long."

"He could still tell R. B. You don't want him to know . . . *yet*."

Thad considered. He took another sip of liquor, then sighed. "You're right, Hurd. Just that I'd have liked Injun Charlie here to know, that's all."

"Too damn much has already been said. Let it go."

"All right, fine," Thad said irritably, and looked at Breck. "You know what to do."

Breck swallowed his drink and tossed the empty glass into one of the stuffed chairs. "Here, Murph" — he pulled a crumpled length of rope from his pants pocket — "cut it in two and tie their hands behind them. They'll have a couple horses somewhere nearby, I reckon. They can tell us where the nags are."

Gage stared frozenly at Thad. "What do you

have planned for us?"

"It's what Uncle Bob will have planned." Thad laughed shortly. "Give you a hint. Ask R. B. what he did to some fuzzie wuzzies once when he was in Africa."

What in the hell does that mean? Gage wondered.

Thad's gaze had already shuttled back to Breck. "You'll set out at first light for the high country. I've told you where the place is. And Pokey will guide you."

"Yes, sir. We'll find it, all right."

"And Breck . . ." Thad paused meaningfully. "You'll tell my uncle just as much as I told you to. No more."

CHAPTER SEVENTEEN

After they had taken Breck and his men to where they'd left the horses, the animals were led back to RBJ headquarters and put up in the stable. Gage and Opal were bedded down in a spare room of the main house, their hands still tied at their backs. The youth called Murph was left in the room, slacked in a chair, to guard them while they tried to sleep.

They caught about three hours apiece. Then they were rousted awake by Breck and his men and brought out to the stable where their own mounts were waiting, saddled and bridled. So were five RBJ horses. The prisoners' bonds were removed and their hands retied in front of them so they could handle their reins. Then Gage and Opal were hoisted onto their saddles.

It was still very early, but enough gray light of coming dawn showed for the party of riders to make their way almost due east across a grassy plain. They rode in a tight bunch, Breck, Pokey, and another of Breck's men ahead of Gage and Opal, and the other two men behind them.

They were taking no chances with their prisoners. The whole operation, from start to finish, had been as beautifully orchestrated as a ballet,

Gage thought with grudging admiration. No doubt Breck's hard-bitten experience had contributed to its success as much as any ideas offered by Overmile or Tancred.

Gage wondered with a bleak fatalism what lay ahead for them. All he'd learned so far indicated that R. B. Janeece was a fanatically dedicated hunter of animals. Then that half-cryptic reference of Thad's to "fuzzie wuzzies in Africa" — what did that mean?

He already had an ominous inkling. But if true, it was hard to believe. . . .

Scatters of buildings here and there, seen at a distance, informed him of the presence of quite a few small settlers in this area. That meant that by now they had passed across the east boundary line of RBJ range. Gage made a careful inspection of the country roundabout as they rode, for his roamings had never taken him this far southeast.

Now they were climbing into the foothills, where the plains grass thinned away and the heights were cowled with a scanty growth of pine and juniper. It thickened into heavy woods as they moved on and upward.

Pokey guided them along the deep-worn trench of an old trail that led upward on a steep incline. No doubt both animals and Indians had used it for a long time, perhaps for centuries.

Finally they came out on a thickly forested flat and pushed through the trees in an even more southerly direction. Pokey led them toward a spiral of smoke that showed above the treetops. Shortly they entered a broad clearing where a rude bivouac was set up, the smoke rising from a campfire near its center.

Two men were standing by the fire, alert to their coming.

One was R. B. Janeece; Gage had seen him once or twice from a distance. He was trim and active-looking, his face seasoned and leathery behind his spruce white mustache. His canvas togs showed the creases and grime of hard wear.

One glance at his companion was enough to give a body a case of the heebie-jeebies; he looked like something out of a bad dream. This would be the Patchwork Man, of whom Gage had occasionally heard but had never seen.

Both men had guns out but relaxed on seeing their visitors.

"Welcome, lads!" Janeece said in a jubilant tone. He waved a hand toward the freshly butchered hide of a huge grizzly stretched on the ground. "I said I'd fetch this big bastard, and I did, early this morning. Now . . . what have we here?"

Breck and his men got off their horses and helped Gage and Opal dismount. The two stood flexing their stiff muscles, while Breck gave R. B. a meager explanation that nevertheless pretty well covered everything, except for that hidden piece of business at which Thad had hinted. Janeece's smile slowly faded and finally turned to a disapproving frown. But he said nothing until Breck had finished.

"That's a damned sorry business," he said slowly. "About the nigger man and the baby."

"Like I said, sir. Mr. Overmile and me didn't have no choice. Darky tried a play with his long gun and we had to dust him. We're covered with the law, and that's all that —"

"Very well," Janeece cut Breck off impatiently. "The job is done. So *that* plan of Hurd's worked, eh? And you've got these two in hand. . . ."

"Mr. Overmile allowed you might want 'em brought here, sir. Said something about 'fuzzie wuzzies,' if that means aught."

Janeece's face altered back to pleasantry. "Did he, then? Thoughtful of Thad. You and your boys may go home now — all except the Indian. I believe I can use him. A man you advised Tancred to hire on, isn't he, Mr. Breck?"

"Yes, sir. We call him Pokey. Not that he is, you understand. He's damn good on track and he moves fast. We just call him that. He can understand our lingo all right."

"Very good. He'll stay."

The other men mounted up, and Breck tapped a finger to his hat brim in farewell. They rode away into the trees.

"Patchy," Janeece said, "strip the gear off our guests' horses. Then turn them out with our own. And see that you hobble them."

The Patchwork Man didn't say a word. Maybe he was incapable of speech. He simply did as told, piling Gage's and Opal's and the Pima's saddle and other gear on the ground. Then, leading the three horses, he led them away through the trees.

"Sit." R. B. looked at Gage and Opal; he motioned toward the fire. "Sit down, please. You, too, my redskinned friend. We're about to have our midday meal. I hope you're hungry."

Pokey grunted; Gage and Opal said nothing. The three of them sat down by the fire, crossing their legs tailor-fashion.

The Patchwork Man returned. He had already prepared a kettle of stew, topped by a cover of sourdough biscuits, and now he hung it on a stick tripod over the flames. He filled a battered coffeepot with water, added some Triple X, and set it down next to the fire.

Janeece sat opposite the others and eyed them almost humorously for a long moment before he spoke again.

"As to Mr. Breck's comment about fuzzie wuzzies. Do either of you know what he meant?"

Both Gage and Opal remained silent and expressionless, although Gage knew. He suspected that Opal did, too.

"They're a wavy-haired black people who inhabit an eastern district of northeast Africa, between the Nile, the Athava River, and the Red Sea. The Haden Dowa is the name they give themselves. But they're called fuzzie wuzzies by the Arabs and are themselves Muslims, although they mingle that creed with older tribal beliefs. War and feuding and making raids against enemies are among their prime traditions."

Janeece extracted a cigar from his breast pocket, lit it from the fire, and puffed out an idle smoke ring. "A few years ago, when Patchy here and I were out hunting with a party of British friends, we chanced on a raiding party of the Haden Dowa. They wanted to fight, and we were happy to oblige them. We wiped them out to a man, except for several who escaped and three we captured. An inspiration popped into my mind. I conveyed it to our British comrades, who, by now, their colonial blood on the rise, and having seen two of their own killed in the encounter, thought it was a jolly good idea."

Janeece grinned from across the fire; he blew another smoke ring. "To make a long story short, we turned them loose, after arming each with a knife. That would be their sole defense. Then we gave them an hour's head start and proceeded to hunt them down. Needless to say, we succeeded in short order."

Gage spoke for the first time, tonelessly. "You killed other men. You hunted them down and killed them like animals."

"Well, of course, young fellow." Janeece gestured idly with the cigar. "We considered them legitimate prey — the lesser breed within the law. And the situation offered an irresistible challenge. Why not? Man hunts every other species of animal on earth . . . quite aside from whether he needs the meat or is killing in self-defense. Otherwise he kills only for the pleasure of the kill. Certainly *I* do."

166

R. B. jerked out a chuckle. "Man, after all, by virtue of his superior intelligence, is supposed to be the most dangerous animal on earth. He's proved it often enough down through the ages, with his genocidal wars, his inquisitions, his witch hunts. I'm willing, at least, to give my human prey a sporting chance."

Gage felt a nerve of quiet shock touched by the man's calm and untroubled cynicism. Maybe he was even more shocked by the answering response he felt within himself. For in a way, from his own perspective anyway, Janeece was only telling the raw truth.

"So," Gage said quietly, "you'll give us a knife, I reckon? Against your rifles and horses. That's your idea of a sporting chance?"

"Tut-tut. I'll do better than that," R. B. said generously. "I'll give *each* of you, you and the ebon lady, a knife."

"And of course an hour's head start?"

"Certainly. The only rifle used on you will be my own. Patchy and Pokey, although armed, will merely serve as my beaters. Unless you provoke them unnecessarily, they will only drive you into a corner. And nobody will pursue you on horseback."

"Then you'll kill us," Gage murmured.

"You had it right the first time, my boy," Janeece said affably. "I'll *hunt* you down. I prefer that way of looking at it. It should serve as the crowning thrill of my career. You see" — R. B. stabbed the cigar at him like a knife — "those fuzzie wuzzies didn't really present much of a challenge. Usually their people follow a nomadic way of life, wandering over wide distances, following their flocks of sheep, their herds of cattle and camels, on whose produce of milk and butter and meat they almost entirely subsist. They know nothing of survival in a heavily forested region."

He paused. "You, on the other hand, are a North American Indian — or at least half of one. You were reared in these parts, so I've heard. I expect you to offer a *true* challenge."

"I'd about figured as much," Gage said dryly. "But you'll give us a hearty meal first, eh?"

"Absolutely! I wouldn't want you to succumb to weakness too early in the game."

Soon the coffee was ready, and a while later the stew was at least partly cooked. The Patchwork Man ladled it onto tin plates for them. Both Gage and Opal were ravenous by then; they wolfed their portions down, eating awkwardly with their bound hands.

Janeece smilingly declined to eat right away; he would prefer, he said, to let the remaining mess of stew cook a while longer. Damned if he'd eat it half-raw, like any *savage*. He sat on his heels, watching them with a serene and disdainful half smile, holding his rifle across his knees.

By the time they had finished eating, the afternoon was half-gone. Janeece gave an order. The Patchwork Man cut away the ropes on Gage's and Opal's hands; he handed each of them a hunt-

168

ing knife while Janeece held his rifle trained on them.

Gage massaged feeling back into his wrists as he said to Janeece, "If I were you, I wouldn't trust either of those two. Your nephew or Hurd Tancred."

"Why so?"

"I don't know. Your nephew said something in front of me and Mrs. Bedoe before Tancred told him to shut up. I couldn't tell what was meant. That's all."

R. B. Janeece threw back his head and gave a full bray of a laugh. "Why, I've never trusted anyone very far, including those two. Also including you, breed. How do I know *you're* telling the truth now? I'll look out for my own interests."

He palmed out his watch and glanced at it. "Now — if I were you, I'd get moving at once. An hour's start, remember? And you're already using it up."

CHAPTER EIGHTEEN

Gage Cameron and Opal Bedoe headed roughly northwest into the thick timber, plunging through the underbrush as fast as they could, making no effort to hide their tracks. Not knowing the country, Gage was looking for a likely point at which to bring his woods lore into play.

He found it at a spot where the pines grew so tall and huge that their densely needled tops almost completely blotted out all but a faint freckling of sunlight, allowing their lower branches to die and practically no underbrush to grow on the forest floor.

They paused. It was like standing in a big, windless cathedral, and the silence all around them was overpowering.

Opal looked about. She whispered in a half-awed tone, "Now what?"

"Now," Gage said, "we strike off at a right angle. You see the ground here? The heavy fall of needles from above has covered it."

"Yes."

"All right. No animal, including us, leaves much of any sign when it crosses a stretch like this. Could throw óff even a Pima Indian for a while. If we're careful, we can cut away from this place somewhere to the side. Will take 'em a while to find out where, and then pick us up again."

"Then . . . we can't really lose them."

"Maybe not. I don't know these parts at all. Likely at least one of them does. But we can buy some time for ourselves. We can keep ahead of them a good while yet."

"And then?" Opal asked.

"We'll know that when we come to it. Let's move."

They crossed sideways over the gold-brown carpet of pine needles, moving slowly and carefully. Again they had to enter heavy timber, and now they went slowly, trying to leave as little of a sign as possible.

Gage led them on a deliberate zigzag route, heading always in one general direction for several hundred feet, always keeping three trees lined up at once, in order to hold them on an arrow-straight line. Then he'd strike off along a bewilderingly different course. It would take any pursuer a good while to figure out each sudden turn he made.

Although Gage didn't know the country, he could take his bearings by the sun and keep the two of them on a roughly northeasterly course. Eventually it would bring them out on familiar ground and then he could make for home as fast as possible.

Opal seemed tireless at first. She was as lithe

as a panther. Following his example as they slithered through brush, she left almost as little of a sign as he did.

The sun was sinking deeply west, and they would have to stop for the night. And safely, for the pursuers would have to stop even sooner, as the dimming light would make tracking impossible.

Gage led the way down the steep-sided inclines of several ravines they had to cross. He'd follow their rough, narrow bottoms for a time, then lead Opal out where the going was easiest, or where the slopes were so rough that they'd leave almost no sign.

Yet, given Janeece's fierce appetite for the hunt, they were bound to be followed relentlessly before they got home free. R. B. Janeece and the Patchwork Man would be old hands at this sort of thing. And the Pima would be no slouch on trail either.

Moreover, Opal was beginning to show signs of exhaustion, though she never uttered a word of complaint. They'd both need the rest that a few hours' halt and sleep could give them.

Gage felt a drain on his own strength as the sun finally slid below the horizon. Maybe a lot of it was just nervous strain. But he was glad enough to see the sun vanish. That would halt the pursuers. And he and Opal could keep pressing on for a while in the same direction until twilight cut off the welter of horizon red where the sun had gone down.

Afterward they wouldn't be able to go on for a time. He could follow such direction as the constellations indicated, but blundering along in the dark through brush and timber would be both uncertain and hazardous.

Darkness was starting to settle when Gage finally called a halt in a small, tree-flanked clearing. Here, if they'd had matches, they could have built a fire without the pursuit party picking up the sight of it. But the Pima at least could possibly smell even a drifting trace of smoke.

Opal was dead tired by now. She dropped to the ground, sitting down and pulling her knees up to her chin. "Lord," she murmured. "I thought I was a tough woman. But I'm all in."

"It's getting to me, too." Gage sank on his haunches facing her. "We need some sleep. I'll take the watch."

"You need sleep, too."

"I can dog it through."

"No. We can take turns on watch."

He didn't reply, and this struck a nerve of pride in her.

"*I* can," Opal said, coolly insistent. "When I've had my bit of sleep, you'll wake me up for my turn."

Gage let out his breath in a gusty sigh. "All right. Agreed. But we've still a ways to go. I don't know just how far until we reach familiar terrain."

"And then we head for your family's place."

"Right. A temporary haven, anyway. Once I have my hands on a gun or two, it'll be *my* game."

"Ours."

"Sure." He smiled wryly in the near-darkness. "And after that —"

"There's young Overmile. I'll still get him, Gage. I swear I will."

"So you believe."

"I *know*."

"Or you'll die trying."

"Yes."

Gage wasn't inclined to hash over that matter again. A man might as well try to butt down a steel door as try to dent Opal Bedoe's determination.

The darkness around was alive with the noises of nocturnal insects and animals. Gage's senses were attuned to these, singling out the sounds almost unconsciously and assessing them.

"Good thing the weather's been fairly seasonable," he said conversationally. "We won't get too cold even by night."

"I suppose that's a piece of luck," Opal said. "But you still believe they'll catch up, don't you?"

"Just a feeling in my bones. You'd best get some sleep now. . . ."

Long before sunrise, when there was just enough smudged light to make their way onward, they struck out again, doggedly, in the same general direction. They weren't much refreshed by the few hours' stop, but Gage had the feeling they weren't far from country familiar to him. After the last stars washed out of the sky, they'd have to halt once more and await the flare of coming dawn . . . and get direction again.

There were several more ravines to be negotiated. As they were climbing out of the third one, Gage guiding them up a tall bank of crumbling rock, a chunk of insecure ledge broke and caved away as Opal set foot on it.

She tumbled helplessly down in a small landslide, trying to hook her fingers into the bank to slow her descent. But it didn't help. She slid clear to the bottom, then raised her face. It was twisted with pain.

He scrambled down to her side. "You're hurt —"

"I'm afraid that I've wrenched my ankle. Badly."

The fixed fatalism that Gage had felt earlier was suddenly and unexpectedly justified. He helped her to her feet, feeling her agonized shudder as she placed her weight on the injured leg.

"Can you walk, do you think?"

"Not far and not fast," she said hopelessly. "Not even with your help. Oh, God. I'm sorry, Gage."

"Not your fault," he said. "I stood on that same ledge. It just happened. Something like this coming about never crossed my mind."

"But you *thought* something would go awry. It did."

"Yeah." Gage scrubbed a hand across his brow.

"Well, that's it. We'll have to make our stand close to here. Wait for them to come up on us . . ."

He tramped a little farther up the arroyo, looking for a better place to climb out. The banks were steep all along the way, but he finally came on a spot where the west side of the ravine slanted upward somewhat less precariously. He doubted they would come on any better place to ascend unless they proceeded a lot farther.

Gage went back to Opal and helped her stand up. He took the burden of her weight against his right side and shoulder. She assisted him as well as she could with her good leg. Reaching the place he had chosen for the ascent, he helped her climb the tall bank. It took them nearly five minutes, with Gage digging his feet against the crumbling rubble, to reach the top.

Here they sat and rested, their legs dangling over the rim, while Gage scanned all the terrain around them. At their backs was a heavy growth of forest and brush. Southward lay the upslanting ravine floor that Janeece and his men must follow as they continued to pick up the track.

He and Opal had some time to spare before they would be overtaken. How much, he had no idea. But maybe enough time to set up a few makeshift preparations. In the end it probably wouldn't make any difference. But now they had no choice at all if they were to survive. It would be kill or be killed, with all odds running against them.

Again Gage helped Opal to her feet. He half carried her back from the rim and into the deepest brush he could find, perhaps a hundred yards away from the ravine. Here he eased her to the ground on her back and knelt down beside her.

"Stay right here," he told her. "Keep flat on the ground. Don't move and don't make a sound, whatever you hear happening."

"Lord . . ." Opal's eyes were dull with pain. "Gage, I —"

"Don't say again that you're sorry. I've cast my lot with yours. My choice."

"Well . . . yes. But —"

"No buts. That's how it's been. From the first, I reckon."

She placed a hand over his and pressed it. "All right. But, Lord — I'm so thirsty."

"So am I, ma'am, but we don't have anything to drink. Just stay here and be quiet and keep low, understand?"

She nodded and forced her dark lips to a smile, her eyes full of trust. Gage doubted that it was really justified, but it helped steel him for whatever might come next.

Now he rose to his feet and headed back the way they had come, through the surrounding trees and brush.

CHAPTER NINETEEN

Shoved into Gage's belt were the two hunting knives that had been given them. By now he had a fairly good idea of how he intended to make use of the weapons.

At a point about a hundred feet from the ravine they had quit, he struck off from the trail he had backtracked and went in a widely variant direction. He left enough sign for R. B. Janeece and his companions to follow easily — but not trying to be too obvious about it.

Gage judged that once the pursuing men had tracked them this far, they would be confused by the divided trails. Likely R. B. would be suspicious of just why the main trail had split apart, but he'd have to assume that from here Gage and Opal had gone their own separate ways. He'd have no choice but to split his own force in order to get them. He and one of his men would have to follow one track while the third man picked up on the other.

That, at least, was Gage's hope. He was sure he couldn't take on all three of them at the same time and hope to stay alive.

He worked into the woods and brush for a short distance, then took one of the knives from his belt and rigged a trap.

Offside of where he had broken track, he found a short tree whose lowest branch projected across the trail. He sheared it clean of twigs and leaves. Then he lashed the knife crosswise near its end, cutting a strip from his shirt for the purpose. He bent the bough back horizontally and placed a dead bough, crotched at one end, in an angle to the ground so that the butt end was dug into the loam. The crotched tip held the branch in a back-bent position.

The slightest touch on that branch would dislodge its small restraint, and the knife would swing out to strike whatever dislodged it.

Gage made his way a little farther forward through the brush, then swung around and, being careful to avoid his own trap, retraced his steps to where he'd split the trail. He headed back to where he'd left Opal.

He didn't go very far. Veering off trail from the slightly broken brush, he cut down a tall sapling. He chopped all the limbs off it and trimmed the ends, then cut another length of cloth from his shirt and secured his second knife to the thicker end of it.

That done, he went swiftly on to where Opal Bedoe lay concealed in the deep brush. She was awake and seemed to be resting quietly.

"How are you doing?" he asked.

"Okay . . . I guess. Are you ready for them now?"

"Ready as I'm likely to be. I'll tell you all

about it later. You just rest some more. Wait."

Again Gage backtracked himself, but this time only for a short distance. Inside the bank of shrubbery alongside the trail he crouched down, laying his improvised spear at his side. He tried to wait with the stolid patience that anyone with Indian blood in him was supposed to have.

Did he have it? He didn't know. All he was dead sure of was that his guts were crawling with tension. His own skilled woodcraft was pitted against the trained skills of his pursuers . . . and he could hope to come out ahead only by an eyelash.

Squatting in a lax and somnolent position, Gage nearly dozed off a few times during the next hour or so. One hour, perhaps two hours. He didn't know how much time had passed.

But finally he heard the sounds of the men on track.

Now they were only a brief distance away. He couldn't make out what they were saying, but he could tell that they had halted and were discussing the confusing split trail.

Then silence . . .

he was sure that, as he'd anticipated. Ja   divided his party. One of the men was c   is way. Gage half rose, his make-shift spea   ready. The Patchwork Man came into sight, plowing almost noiselessly through the brush with an alert but deadly intent.

Gage rose fully to his feet and flung the spear

with all his strength. As he did so, the Patchwork Man half turned, whipping his rifle to his shoulder.

But Gage's spear struck before the Patchwork Man could open fire. More by chance than by intent, the blade drove hard and deep into his left eye. Into his brain. The Indian took a single wobbling step more, then fell forward on his face.

Gage sprang out of cover and grabbed up the man's rifle. At once, feeling it solid in his hands, he felt a rush of self-assurance. He made a hasty check of the Winchester repeater and found that the weapon was fully loaded. He was almost on even terms with the others — except that he was one man to their two.

Gage hurried on, half running, to where he had falsely divided the trails. He followed the other trail now, moving quickly and silently.

He heard a sudden half yelp of pain from just ahead — and knew that one of them, either Janeece or the Pima, had run into his other trap. One of them had tripped the waiting knife held back on a branch, having come up on it too late to see it.

Gage ran fast. He came on them suddenly. The Pima huddled on the ground, R. B. Janeece crouching beside him, peering warily around.

Gage quickly cocked back the hammer of his Winchester just as Janeece caught sight of him. Gage hardly took the time to draw an aim before he fired.

Janeece was already bringing his express rifle

up. But Gage's bullet slammed him in the chest an instant before the other man pulled the trigger. Janeece's rifle went off before it was leveled, firing downward. The blast knocked him off his feet. He was flung over backward, crashing into the brush. The branches settled slowly under his weight and then dumped him almost gently to the ground underneath.

Gage levered a second cartridge into the Winchester's chamber and moved cautiously forward. A great red stain had splashed across the front of Janeece's jacket, but it had ceased to spread as soon as his heart quit. Just that quickly, it was over.

The Pima had dropped his rifle. Now, with one hand grasping his thigh where the knife had hit, he was reaching out in an effort to grab hold of the weapon. Gage walked over and gave the gun a flip with the toe of his moccasin, knocking it well out of his reach.

The Pima sank back, eyeing Gage with the stoic look of a man who thought he was about to die.

Gage shook his head once, side to side. "That's it," he told the Pima. "That's all of it. You fellows lost."

He cut away the Pima's pant leg. Using a stick and Janeece's belt, he applied a tourniquet to Pokey's thigh above his wound and directed him to keep the belt tightly twisted, letting up the pressure now and again to restore circulation. Then Gage cut enough cloth from Janeece's canvas jacket to make a thick pad of bandage that he fastened around the Pima's wound.

"You'll have to make it home by yourself," he told Pokey. "The other one, Patchy, is as dead as the old man here." He paused. "Don't like to just leave you, hurt like you are. But you bought into this. Your own choice."

The Pima was silent. His eyes were like flat black chips of obsidian, showing an enemy nothing. He wouldn't have done the same for Gage if he had been in his place, that was certain.

Gage appropriated Janeece's canteen, his small knapsack of provisions, and a couple of blankets. He looked at the Pima's water bottle, fashioned from the gut of a horse or a mule, and decided to leave that with him.

Standing up now, Gage gave Janeece's body an indifferent glance.

CHAPTER TWENTY

After giving Opal some water and a small amount of food, Gage inspected her wrenched ankle. The flesh was hard, hot, and swollen, and likely it would get worse.

He bound more of the cloth ripped from Janeece's jacket to make a thick and very tight wrapping around her leg. It would help support her if she had to put her weight on it again inadvertently. She probably would, as some irregular and ravine-slashed country remained between here and his own territory. Crossing over it, hardly anybody could keep from stumbling now and again.

Gage further tried to minimize the problem by devising a crude crutch for Opal. He cut down another sapling and trimmed it, leaving a Y-shaped crotch to brace her underarm while he supported her on the other side.

They set out on their original course once more, not being in any particular hurry now. No need to worry about anyone from the RBJ outfit catching up before the Pima could make his way back and tell them what had happened.

That's if they even wanted to bother. Thad Overmile and Hurd Tancred had been conspiring against Janeece in some way. They had said just enough, Gage thought, for him to assume that they'd be glad to have him out of the way — and no questions asked.

By midafternoon he and Opal reached familiar country. Now he could move along faster, avoiding the rugged places, sticking with ease to the old trails long known to him.

Sundown.

By now they weren't far from his home place, but both of them were exhausted. They made camp, and Gage broke out a little more water and provisions. Afterward they both stretched out on the bare ground and slept the sleep of the dead.

But we're not dead yet, was his last thought before he drifted off. Maybe we'll both make it through all this.

Both of them were so used up that, on awakening close to dawn, he decided to let Opal sleep for as long as she could. He ate his share of the remaining provisions and sat patiently, waiting. An hour or so after sunrise, she sat up suddenly in her blankets, looking wildly around. Seeing him close beside her, she relaxed with a drowsy sigh.

"Want to rest a while longer?" he asked with the hint of a smile.

"No!" A visible shudder ran through her. "Let's go on at once. We're close to your home, didn't you say?"

"Pretty close. I've eaten. You wrap yourself around the last of the grub and water with which Mr. Janeece has so considerately supplied us. Then we'll get along. . . ."

They reached the Cameron headquarters about noon.

Opal had wondered about how she, a black woman, might be accepted by Gage's people. He'd assured her there was no cause for concern. In some ways he didn't understand his own family any better than they understood him. But on this score he had no doubts about them at all, and he was right.

All three of them, Mungo, Ran, and Amber, were waiting in the yard as Gage and Opal came tottering unsteadily into the clearing outside the cabin. Both Mungo and Ran had pistols in their hands, as if they were riding a tight edge and didn't know quite what to expect.

Opal was glaze-eyed by now; she looked dully around her and then at the Cameron trio, uncomprehendingly.

Amber said softly and sympathetically, "Oh, God. That poor woman!" She came quickly forward to take Opal's sagging weight from Gage's tired hold and help her into the cabin.

Gage stood where he was, swaying a little on his feet, staring in a stupor of fatigue at his father and Ran. Could they actually have been waiting for him out of concern? Old Mungo, for a wonder, seemed to be dead sober. And Ran wasn't out

186

roaming or hunting, as one would expect of him.

"Come now, laddie," Mungo said gruffly, and walked over to grasp his son's arm. "Let's go inside."

Ran followed them into the cabin. Gage slacked down on a bench at the table. Amber took Opal into her own room and helped the exhausted woman lie down, then drew a blanket over her. Returning to the common room, Amber dished up a cold meal and hot coffee for Gage.

He ate ravenously, looking up from his plate now and then at his kinfolk. The three of them had seated themselves on the bench opposite him, eyeing him intently.

What the hell's happened here? Gage wondered. He'd never seen them look just so. But he said nothing.

Finally old Mungo spoke. "Soon as you care to, would you kindly tell us what's passed with you?"

"Not a hell of a lot," Gage said between mouthfuls of food, his tone only mildly sarcastic.

"Like hell," Ran said gently. "Suppose you tell us about all of it. We're fair, champing at the bit, Chief."

The edge was off Gage's appetite, and he ate slowly as he finished up his food. Meantime he told them in a general way what had happened since he had last seen them. By the time he was done eating and was on his third cup of coffee, he felt pretty well talked out.

"Mrs. Bedoe is welcome under our roof."

Mungo made a wide embracing gesture with both his arms. "But, lad, from what you've said, you may have shook up a considerable hornet's nest for all of us."

"Reckon that's so, Pa." Gage finished his coffee and set the cup down, lifting a sardonic brow. "And what's passed with *you?*"

"How d'you mean?"

"You're stark sober and it's already afternoon. First time I can recall that happening in a score of Sundays."

Mungo Cameron brushed a hand over his beard, not scowling too much. "Aye. Well . . . all of us got worrying about your vagabond hide. So I stayed sober, and Ran here stayed at home."

Ran grinned. "That's right, Chief. Believe it or don't."

"Aye," Mungo half growled. "Before now, you've gone off alone for untimely spells. But for some reason I can't name, I had a bad feeling about it this time. So did Randolph. Still, we had no idea what to do. So we decided to stay right smack here and wait on you."

Gage only nodded, hiding how strongly warmed he felt by the old man's words. "Anyway, Pa . . . it's as I've told you. We're rich people now."

"I am still trying to soak all that up," Mungo said slowly. "So it's straight goods, eh? About this huge trove of gold you found?"

"True as Gospel," Gage said soberly. "Half-breed speak with straight tongue, Pa."

Mungo continued to scowl, but he rubbed a

hand over his mouth as if to conceal a grin, and his eyes kindled with glints of amusement. "Very well. But it's *your* gold, laddie. You discovered it. Why wait till now to tell us?"

"Maybe for the same reason you three suddenly got concerned about me. Meaning I don't know for sure. But . . . I meant to set aside an amount for Ran's schooling, and Amber's. To serve as their introduction to the outside world, you might say. I wasn't sure how to go about it . . . or if they'd let me do it."

Ran grinned and shrugged, then glanced at his sister. "Maybe we ought to let him. What d'you think, sis?"

A slight flush tinted Amber's face. She looked down at her hands, folded on the tabletop. "I guess I'll go along with that. See, Gage, Ran and me talked it out at considerable length over the past couple days. I don't know why; we just did. This was right after what happened over by the Swimhole . . . but you wouldn't know about that."

Gage said no and felt a gratified pleasure as Ran and Amber, between them, told about the whole incident by the river. By the time they were done, he was joining in their laughter.

"What did you do with the possessions he left?" Gage asked.

"Well," Ran said, "we tied his pants and boots on his saddle, shoved his long iron in the saddle sheath, and turned his critter loose. Reckon it got back to its home range all right. But jeez,

Gage, it was really funny. You should've seen ol' Thad hopping away across that ledge and diving into the river and getting washed away! I hustled him along with a few more shots."

"You would," Gage said, still chuckling. "But I'm curious as to why this sudden change came over you two."

"I don't know for sure, Gage," Amber said. "It just did. Ran and me got to talking, and it developed we'd both got thinking we'd been too wild and willful. We figured that if we kept doing it much longer, it could land both of us in a real pickle. Isn't that right, Ran?"

"That's about it, Chief." Ran nodded.

Mungo cleared his throat, hacking loudly. "We're still in deadly danger. If old Janeece is dead and the RBJ folks know you got away, they might come here, thinking it's the first place Gage would head for."

Gage shook his head. "I don't think so, Pa."

He enlarged on the enigmatic discussion between Thad and Tancred. Exactly what they'd had in mind he wasn't sure, but it was clear they'd be pleased at having R. B. Janeece out of the way.

"Aye, that's plain," Mungo said. "But why, laddie?"

Gage shook his head. "I don't know. I have a suspicion, though. Ran, maybe you can find out for us. . . ."

CHAPTER TWENTY-ONE

Some hours later Opal was rested enough to join them at supper. Gage's kin were behaving more amiably toward one another and him than he could remember in years. Even Mungo, not having shipped on a load of red-eye for a good while, joined in the usual household badinage, which for once — and for a wonder — wasn't touched with acrimony or rancor.

Moreover they all seemed to have promptly accepted Opal as one of them, quite easily and naturally. No doubt they assumed (and rightly) that Gage had a special interest in her.

She still wasn't up to offering more than small, stiff, remote smiles or one-word replies to their friendly sallies. But all of them understood why this was, and nobody pressed her.

This was important to Gage. He and Opal still had a lot to work out between them, including what course her future would take, before they could really talk on a common ground. That would take a good deal of time, with the memories still fresh and bleeding in her mind.

Everything had happened too fast; so much was still uncertain. Even if Ran and Amber were in earnest about wanting to pursue a different way of life, what assurance did he have that either would stick with the decision? None. Any more than he could be sure that his father wouldn't resume his steady intake of booze — even if Mungo vigorously declared, while they were eating, that he was shoving the cork in the bottle for good.

That sort of hot-off-the-griddle resolution was cheap coin in which to trade. What people might say one day could change overnight. Still it was all that Gage could go on, or believe in, for now.

He and Opal talked a good deal over the next few days.

She frankly admitted that she wasn't in a condition either mentally or physically to make any sense even to herself. Her remarks were vague and disconnected; her thoughts seemed to wander. Otherwise she appeared to be recovering pretty well. Maybe their terrorized flight from Janeece and his men had branded itself on her mind as much as had her hot obsession for revenge against Thad Overmile.

So Gage skirted carefully around the subject. But he sensed that she hadn't given up on Overmile, and he still doubted that she ever would.

Meantime, at Gage's request, Ran had gone out daily to check on what he could learn about Thad Overmile's current activities. What he reported back confirmed Gage's suspicions.

When he'd been swept downriver, Overmile must have discovered the site where Gage had

192

extracted the gold-bearing ore. For by now Over-mile had a crew of men working the cliffside, digging out more. From the feverish activity, Ran — spying on them from a distance — guessed that they must be reaping a fortune.

Gage did not really care. In a single night he'd taken out enough gold to comfortably supply himself and his family for many years. Even the horses that he and Opal had left in Janeece's camp had strayed back to the Cameron range, no doubt turned loose by RBJ crewmen, who must have gone to the camp and liberated them. The Hurteen brothers had found the animals on-range and had fetched them to headquarters. Damned considerate of the RBJ boys. Perhaps it was a truce signal of sorts: You let us alone and we'll let you alone.

That was damned satisfactory to Gage. But he couldn't believe it would satisfy Opal. Again, he was correct.

On the morning of the fourth day, after Opal joined the Camerons at breakfast, she suddenly turned to him, saying flatly, "I'm still going to get him, Gage. I'm going to get that damned Overmile. Even if I don't get anybody else."

Gage turned a chunk of griddle cake around in his mouth, chewing slowly. "Yeah. You've scaled your ambitions down a bit."

"What do you mean?"

"Before, you wanted to do in three of them. Now it's just Overmile."

Her face softened its hard edges; she reached out a hand and laid it on his. "It's all right. My mind is working fine now. But I have to do *this*. Overmile was the real instigator."

"All right. Under two conditions."

"What?"

"I'm going along with you. All the way to the end of the line. Understood?"

She curved her fingers around his hand and pressed it tighter yet. That was all the reply he needed.

"How 'bout me lending a hand?" Ran asked.

Gage shook his head. "Stay out of it. This is our business, hers and mine. The rest of you are too much involved already."

Opal said, "What's the other condition, Gage?"

"I told you about our great-uncle, Adakhai."

"Yes. You feel that he has . . . powers of some kind."

Gage nodded. "I want to take you to him first. Hear what he has to say."

Opal hesitated only a moment. "Very well."

Gage and Opal set out for Adakhai's camp. They crossed one heavily brushed ridge. Then Opal, who had been warily studying their back trail as they rode, said suddenly, "Gage, someone is trailing us. I saw him for just a moment atop that ridge we came over."

Gage smiled. "Right. That'll be Ran. He's following us at a distance. I thought he would."

"But you told him —"

194

"Not to. It won't matter. He'll do what suits him. We Camerons are like that, damned independent. Ran will look for a chance to help us if he can. But after what I said to him, he'll keep a ways behind us."

They crossed another ridge and came down into the shallow valley where Adakhai and his near-relatives lived. Again Gage was greeted by two of the old man's granddaughters. who clapped their hands over their mouths in astonishment at the sight of Opal. Obviously they'd never seen a woman of her darkness before.

As on Gage's previous visit, Adakhai sat behind a trench full of banked fire coals. He motioned them to sit, and both of them sat down opposite him, crossing their legs tailor-fashion.

"You were expected," the old man said huskily. "You and the woman."

"I thought perhaps we were," Gage said in a moderate tone. "And that you know why we're here, *Hatali*."

"It may be. But tell me, *tineh*. Tell me everything."

Patiently Gage told all that had happened with him since his last visit to Adakhai's lodge.

"*Hoh-hoh*," the ancient medicine man said. "And now you believe?"

Gage smiled faintly. "It is as I have said before. I do not always know what to believe. But you have been right in what you have told me. That much I know. If you will speak of what awaits us, the woman and me, it may be a help. I shall translate your words for her."

Adakhai closed his eyes for a few moments, then opened them. He nodded his head once, up and down. "All will go well for you and the woman if you do only as your hearts tell you."

"That is all?" Gage tried to keep any trace of annoyance out of his voice.

"That is enough. You still wear your *bizha,* your medicine."

"Yes."

"It is well. Do as your medicine bids you. *Remember this.*"

After his visitors had departed. Adakhai used a stick to stir up the coals in the fire trench. Again he closed his eyes and slumped into a trance. Perhaps there was a way he could aid *tineh* and the woman. Perhaps . . .

Visions impinged on his brain as flickering responses to his unspoken prayers. Yes . . . he must invoke the Talking God first of all. Adakhai began to chant in a low voice, his upper body swaying back and forth.

> "Now I walk with Talking God
> With goodness and beauty in all things
> Around me I go.
> With goodness and beauty
> I follow immortality.
> This being, I go. . . ."

It was a fitting prayer, for Adakhai knew that

his own days were drawing to a close. The end was very near. With that propitiation done, he was ready to offer his last invocation.

He prayed fervently, almost fiercely, to the gods of storm. And most of all to Neyenezthan, the god who would strike with four lightnings. . . .

CHAPTER TWENTY-TWO

Thad Overmile, Hurd Tancred, and Breck had pitched in with their crew of ten handpicked men at the job of extracting chunks of ore thickly studded with streaks of solid gold out of the cliffside.

All of them were filled with a keen exultance, and it lent a feverish energy to their work as they continued to dig out the gold, day after day. By now they had unearthed the equivalent of several fortunes, and each man had been assured that he'd receive a generous share of the final take.

The crew of workers was split in half. Five men stationed up on the rimrock let themselves down on ropes securely fastened to massive boulders. Each man had a hatchet; they whacked away steadily at the exposed earth of the cliff wall, cascading big chunks of ore to the ribbon of riverbank below.

At the base of the cliff, the other men stood well out of the way as the sections of earth, ore, and gold came thudding down. Then a halt was called, and the men above left off work to let the men below sort and gather up the ore.

Thad, Tancred, and Breck, working in unison,

swiftly stowed the best of the stuff into heavy canvas bags and passed these along to the five crewmen stationed beside them. These men shouldered the bags and carried them upriver along the narrow sloping bank beside the roiling rapids. When they came to the shallows, they could slog across to the far shore, where they could dump their burdens to the ground on RBJ's main property.

Just now the men bearing the ore had departed on their upriver trek. Thad, Tancred, and Breck edged out of the way, and Thad signaled the five men above to resume digging.

A pleasant day to be getting the work done. The sky was a cleanly scoured blue, and dazzling sunlight poured out of it. Probably the last day they would be occupied with the task, for the heavily gold-laden ore was showing signs of starting to peter out. But that was all right, Thad thought, feeling in a pretty sunny mood himself.

He wiped sweat from his face onto his sleeve, then squatted down on the slender bank and glanced cheerfully at Tancred and Breck. "Sit down, fellows. Let's have a smoke. Well, we're rich men now, eh? How does it feel?"

Thad offered each of them a cigar. Tancred accepted one, but Breck politely refused; he preferred to roll a cigarette and did so. Thad struck a match and lit his and Tancred's cigars, then held the match out to Breck, who again demurred.

"Three on a match," he murmured. "There's

them say that's asking for the worst kind o' luck, Mr. Overmile."

Thad pulled his arm back with a mild chuckle; the breath of it blew out the match. "Rank superstition, Breck. I'm not a superstitious man."

Breck's flat, slate-colored eyes showed nothing at all. "Neither am I, sir. Just that I been a heap of places in my time and have seen things I wouldn't want to take head-on against me.

"I dunno for sure. . . ." Breck nodded upward at the cliffside. "But I keep an ear cocked always. Man learns to do that if he keeps alive long as I have. I heard some strange things, hither and yon, about this place. Take that ol' Navaho village back a ways above here. Talk says it's haunted. That the ol' spirits have got a spell set on this place."

Thad grinned easily. "Talk's cheap. But no reasoning man would believe such rot. Would he, Hurd?"

Tancred puffed on his cigar, his eyes hooded. "I reckon not. Leastways I don't. But a man never knows for sure."

"Hell, man. You're an agnostic. Should have known it, I suppose. You're a pretty careful sort, as a rule."

Tancred's heavy brows drew down. "What's that-there word? Ag . . . ?"

"Agnostic," Thad said, enjoying his edge of knowledge above that of his companions. "A term contrived by a British biologist named Huxley. It derives from the ancient Greek *ag* and *nos*, meaning 'not know.' Refers to one who suspends judgment for lack of evidence."

Tancred nodded slowly, his brows still contracted to a scowl. "That's me, then. You might do well to foller the same notion, Thad."

"Rot!"

"I don't know 'bout none of it," Breck said. He dropped his smoke and stood up, grinding the cigarette under his heel. "It might be a thing to take heed of, Mr. Overmile. Grant you, we're getting a mighty lot o' riches out o' here real fast. It's just I got a bad feeling in my marrow. Sooner we're done with the job, the better I'll like it."

"Well, all right," Thad said tolerantly. "Each to his own. Let's get back to work."

In Thad's view everything was pretty well settled. Uncle Bob was out of the way, as Breck and his men had verified by backtracking to R. B. Janeece's camp with Pokey the Pima and then following the spoor from there. They had come on the bodies of both R. B. and the Patchwork Man and had buried them where they had fallen. Afterward they had taken the two Cameron horses back to the boundary of Cameron range and turned them loose.

Gage Cameron and the nigra wench had escaped, and that was fine with Thad.

Now that R. B. was dead, he had no desire to pursue the business further unless the Camerons wanted to push it. The gesture of returning the horses should let them know it. Thad was satisfied to let it go at that if they were.

Again they stood out of the way, and Thad motioned the men above to knock loose more of the cliffside earth. As it came crashing down, Breck said abruptly, "Look up there. Sky's changing."

So it was. Only a few moments before, the sky had been a bright, clear azure. Now a solid front of dark, roiling clouds was racing out of the north, as if driven by the furies of hell.

"All right," Thad said impatiently. "A storm's coming. What of it? We've all seen storms before."

"Not like this one," Breck said tensely. "She's coming up *against the wind*. You ever see anything like that?"

Tancred glanced at Thad. "Ask the boss here. What d'you say, boss?"

"I say don't talk like a pair of damned fools," Thad snapped. "It's a freak of air currents, nothing more. They run one way down here, another way up there."

"Maybe," Breck said, "we'd all do well to clear out o' here. Now."

"What's that?" Thad said sarcastically. "A hunch you have?"

"That's about it."

"To hell with your hunches!" Thad replied savagely. "I'm the man in charge here, and don't you by God forget it!"

Even as the words left his lips, he saw the

ominous mass of clouds blotting out the sun and staining the sky above them. But only the strip of sky along the men's own position.

With unthinkable quickness rain began to pelt down. Not in a few preliminary drops, but in sudden torrents, literally bucketloads of water smashing down on them.

"All right!" Thad yelled at the men on the cliff. "Clear out, boys. Get up those ropes and onto solid ground. Fast!"

Breck had already dived into the Los Pinos, whose current was carrying him swiftly downriver. Tancred was about to plunge in after him when a big rock, tearing loose from its rain-softened mooring, came bounding down the cliff.

It struck Tancred in the head and crushed his skull to a crimson rain. In the same horrified moment, Thad saw Tancred's body crumple loosely into the water and get swept away.

The whole side of the cliff was coming down in a gigantic slide of mud and rocks. Thad saw the men coming down with it, heard their anguished yells above the roar of falling earth.

Rather than be caught beneath the collapsing cliff, Thad dived into the river, too. He was soon relentlessly bounced and jolted over protruding rocks as he was swept downstream.

CHAPTER TWENTY-THREE

By late afternoon Gage and Opal reined in their mounts at the back of a grassy rise along the east bank of the Los Pinos. From here they could make out the hive of activity on the cliff diggings across the river, perhaps a hundred yards distant. At least five men were suspended from ropes, knocking out chunks of earth as Gage himself had done.

Gage trained his binoculars on the men but couldn't identify any of them. Then he tipped the glasses lower, down to the three men on the narrow margin of bank below.

Overmile. Tancred. Breck.

Wordlessly he handed Opal the field glasses and pointed at the three. She studied them for a long moment, then lowered the glasses.

"All right," she whispered. "I wonder if I could hit him from here?"

"I doubt you're any Annie Oakley," Gage said dryly. "And I couldn't swear to being able to fetch him from this far myself. We'll need to get in closer. Then, if we can bring him down, be prepared to run like hell back to the horses."

The two dismounted and ground-hitched their animals, then slipped their rifles from the saddle boots. They stole up nearer the enemy by skirting around the long rise on its far side. They kept themselves stooped low and clung to the east slope, barely showing their eyes above the angle of ground.

"Look." Opal pulled suddenly to a stop, seizing his arm and pointing upward. "Look, Gage!"

She had seen the phenomenon before he did. Billows of massive dark clouds were churning out of the north. The abruptness with which it occurred was disconcerting enough. But even more eerie, more chilling, was the sight of the clouds massing in an elongated ribbon above this particular point, overhanging the cliff and the river. And it was swarming in *against* the wind . . . while the sky to east and west, north and south, remained a clear and cloudless blue.

Gage felt a terrible coldness ripple along his backbone.

He saw crooked and crackling forks of lightning angle down unevenly from four corners of the boiling sky toward the cliffside.

"What is it?" Opal cried. "Gage!"

Adakhai, he thought, and clasped a hand around his *bizha.* It seemed to glow warmly in his fist, and now memory of the old shaman's last words to him rushed back. He knew what to do.

Gage slipped the thonged amulet off over his head and held it out to her. "Put that on."

"But . . . that's your personal medicine, isn't it?"

"Yes. I want you to have it."

"But —"

"I don't know why, Opal. Just take it."

He could have added that he sensed some Power was protecting him as one of the *Dineh,* that he felt it overwhelmingly, but that she would need the additional protection of his *bizha.* Perhaps that was the last message that Adakhai, in his usual enigmatic way, had conveyed to him. Now, suddenly, it was becoming clear.

Opal dropped the talisman over her neck, just as the dark swirl of clouds opened up, discharging mighty gusts of rain.

They watched it happen. The whole side of the cliff came sliding down in a huge avalanche of mud and rock, taking the men with it, burying them.

They saw Breck dive into the river to escape the crumbling mass. They saw Hurd Tancred falling into the water with a crushed head. Finally Thad Overmile plunged in. And all three bodies tumbled downriver through the creaming, mud-stained rapids.

"Come on!" Gage shouted. "You want him so much, here's your chance!"

They ran toward the river at a slantwise course, hoping to come out at a place where Thad and Breck were able to struggle free of the current. In a few moments Gage and Opal were inside the shroud of icy, punishing rain and were slowing down, trying to sort out details through the slashing murk.

Gage saw two dark figures flounder out of the river on this side. He ran on now, thumbing back the hammer of his rifle. Opal was close at his side, her own rifle ready, and both fired at the same time.

Running over uneven ground, neither scored a hit. The two men hauled up short, then split apart. Breck came on doggedly, his revolver out. He fanned the hammer, emptying his gun at Gage Cameron.

Gage came to a dead stop, bracing his rifle to his shoulder, and fired just once.

Breck folded in his tracks and pitched forward, a reflex pulling of the trigger sending his final shot into the wet ground.

Opal had swung away from Gage, concentrating on Thad Overmile. As he went limping off sideways through the rainy murk, she sent off a shot that caused him to stagger.

He nearly fell but then recovered and came about, swinging on his heels. He was cornered and he knew it, opening fire at Opal with his revolver, making a clean miss. She stopped, planted her feet firmly against the rain-mushed sod, and fired.

She hit him again, but he didn't stop coming. He kept slogging toward her, his tall, strongly built frame lurching from side to side as he bulled onward. Opal pumped two more shots into him, seeing him jerk at the bullets' impact, watching him try to bring up his revolver again, only to have it slip nervelessly from his fingers.

Thad was so close that she could see the pale grimace of his clenched teeth. He threw his arms out as if in a last effort to get his hands on her.

She fired once more, almost point-blank. Overmile toppled on his face, his fingers hooking deep into the muddy soil hardly a foot from her feet.

"It's done," Gage said. "It's all over."

Ran stood nearby, grinning at them. "All sewed up for sure, and I didn't come on fast enough to get in even one shot. Reckon you didn't need me. You two go good together."

Opal stood close beside Gage, huddled against the warmth of his arm around her shoulders.

The storm clouds had frayed away as suddenly as they had appeared. The sun and the azure sky sparkled cloudlessly from one horizon to the other. As if the ancient gods (or spirits or whatever) had vented their final revenge and were satisfied.

Opal turned her glance to his, tears streaming down her face. "I don't feel any better," she whispered. "I got him and I don't feel a whit better for it. God . . . is that all there was to it?"

"I don't know," Gage said slowly. "Maybe, maybe not. But you and I have to go on from here, Opal. People are made that way. They have to go on living."

T.V. Olsen was born in Rhinelander, Wisconsin, where he continued to live all his life. "My childhood was unremarkable except for an inordinate preoccupation with Zane Grey and Edgar Rice Burroughs." He had originally planned to be a comic strip artist but the stories he came up with proved far more interesting to him, and compelling, than any desire to illustrate them. Having read such accomplished Western authors as Les Savage, Jr., Luke Short, and Elmore Leonard, he began writing his first Western novel while a junior in high school. He couldn't find a publisher for it until he rewrote it after graduating from college with a Bachelor's degree from the University of Wisconsin at Stevens Point in 1955 and sent it to an agent. It was accepted by Ace Books and was published in 1956 as HAVEN OF THE HUNTED.

Olsen went on to become one of the most widely respected and widely read authors of Western fiction in the second half of the 20th Century. Even early works such as HIGH LAWLESS and GUNSWIFT are brilliantly plotted with involving characters and situations and a simple, powerfully evocative style. Olsen went on to write such important

Western novels as THE STALKING MOON and ARROW IN THE SUN which were made into classic Western films as well, the former starring Gregory Peck and the latter under the title SOLDIER BLUE starring Candice Bergen. His novels have been translated into numerous European languages, including French, Spanish, Italian, Swedish, Serbo-Croatian, and Czech.

The second edition of TWENTIETH CENTURY WESTERN WRITERS concluded that "with the right press Olsen could command the position currently enjoyed by the late Louis L'Amour as America's most popular and foremost author of traditional Western novels." His novel THE GOLDEN CHANCE (Gold Medal, 1992) won the Golden Spur Award from the Western Writers of America in 1993.

Suddenly and unexpectedly, death claimed him in his sleep on the afternoon of July 13, 1993. His work, however, will surely abide. Any Olsen novel is guaranteed to combine drama and memorable characters with an authentic background of historical fact and an accurate portrayal of Western terrain.

The employees of G.K. HALL hope you have enjoyed this Large Print book. All our Large Print titles are designed for easy reading, and all our books are made to last. Other G.K. Hall Large Print books are available at your library, through selected bookstores, or directly from us. For more information about current and upcoming titles, please call or mail your name and address to:

G.K. HALL
PO Box 159
Thorndike, Maine 04986
800/223-6121
207/948-2962